for. No, he'd been careful, picked out microphones and cameras that a simple search would fail to reveal. His ability to track her car and phone—those were things no small firm would consider, and who else could she have hired? It wasn't as if she knew much of anything about such people and their abilities. No, she'd have gone to the first firm that appeared halfway decent, or more likely, the one her manager recommended, and what did Daniel know about security?

At the end of the day, she would lose her temper with whoever was brought into the house, and the intruder would be gone, removed from his path.

Lily was his, and in time even she would come to accept it.

Shadows of the Past

Chapter One

Harvey Brent gestured to the chair in the small office. "You're looking good."

Michael smiled at his boss and slipped into the chair, feeling the shift of wood and leather beneath his body. The office was a small one, but it suited the older man who ran the business.

"Thanks." Michael met Harvey's gaze before he caught sight of the papers spread out across Harvey's desk. Forms their clients filled in, a few bills—the usual assortment Michael had come to expect. "What's going on?"

"An assignment. New client."

There was always a new client. Security. It was always needed by someone, a business, an individual. Then there were the occasional retrieval jobs Harvey agreed to. Sometimes it would be a person as it had been when Kyle had been sent to collect Lyn from Las Vegas. Other times it would be an item that needed to find its way back to the rightful owner.

"It should be an easy job, Michael. Simple bodyguard work. The assignment is the quiet sort, no family in the area, no boyfriend, she focuses on her work, the deadlines, and—"

"Harvey, you don't have to sell me on something I've already agreed to do. I know under normal circumstances, you'd talk to Kyle about this job, but the guy needs quality alone time. New relationships and all that." Michael leaned back in the chair, his gaze fixed on the older man. Now there was a situation you didn't come across very often; send a man to bring back an unwilling heiress, only to have him fall head-over-heels in love with the woman. He didn't begrudge Kyle his time with Lyn, and the team had learned to cover for each other when personal matters demanded attention. "What's going on? Is there something about this job which could cause a problem?" No job was entirely simple, no matter how it appeared at first glance.

Harvey reached for his mug of coffee, his brow furrowed. The older man paused long enough to take a mouthful from the mug before he set it back down. "It would be easier to explain if you opened the file."

Michael Parker hesitated only a moment before he reached for the manila folder and tugged it off the desk. What in hell's name had gotten into the man? Harvey Brent, founder and owner of Brent's Security, didn't play games, wasn't the type of man to try to reach into the minds of the men and women who worked for him or to toss their brains in a blender and hit frappé.

Harvey gestured to the file and waited for Michael to read through the documents.

Michael opened it and let his gaze move over the first page. A dozen details jumped out at him, from the location of the woman's house to the small studio she occasionally used, the coffee shop she visited daily and the handful of appearances she'd booked. His jaw clenched. Appearances? It was one thing to protect a client within their own home or on the occasional shopping trip, but public events added a new layer of complexity. "She's an artist, isn't she?"

"Yes." Harvey inclined his head. "Talented one, as I understand such things, with most of her income coming in from private commissions."

"Why's she doing the appearances then?" Galleries, perhaps? Yes, it would make sense. Small gatherings he would be able to cope with as long as he had the time to scope the locations out.

"Fan communities, furry conventions, science fiction and fantasy conventions. The usual type of thing," Harvey explained, his tone neutral. "A lot of her commissions are from fan communities, but her work also includes book covers, portraits, web graphics, that type of thing. Some of it's traditional art, though she does a lot of digital painting as well as photo manipulation work, especially for covers."

"Talented." *Conventions.* Michael closed his eyes. Crowds. Perhaps hundreds of people; God alone knew how many people at-

Shadows of the Past

tended these things. Multiple threats from far too many angles of approach. How the hell was one person supposed to deal with the possibilities? What was he expected to do, split himself into a dozen people to protect the woman? He shook himself and met Harvey's gaze. "How many of these conventions is she scheduled for in the coming month?"

"One. Details are three pages in. The client has five panels plus her booth, which will be open in the dealers' hall during normal hours. All a part of the contract she signed with the convention." Harvey leaned back in his chair. "I've already discussed the possibility of backing out, but she's not open to the idea. She doesn't like the idea of disappointing people. Though she pointed out that if she backed out, she might not be invited a second time. A valid concern when you work as a freelancer. I imagine reputation is everything, as it is in our line of work."

Not the same thing. Not like she's saving lives.

"Attendance information?" Michael flipped through the pages. Not invited back to a convention. Would it be such a bad thing? He could discuss the event with the woman when they met. What would she be giving up anyway? A couple of hundred people? Maybe a thousand? He let his gaze focus on the information in the file. "Never mind. Shit, this isn't a small thing. Five thousand attendees?" What the hell was Harvey thinking? Never mind Harvey. What was the woman thinking? Did she believe anyone working with her would be able to pull off the impossible? Any public appearance was a difficult thing to manage. The size of the crowd, multiple exits and entrance points, events where Michael would have to allow others close to his assignment. God, it would be worse than merely close. They'd want to touch her or hug her. Others might want to hand off items to be signed. It all suggested a situation far larger than a single person was capable of managing.

"The numbers are based on average attendance in the last five years, though it doesn't consider all ticket sales to date, and their numbers have increased in the last two years." Harvey gestured to the file. "Lots of costumes, more guests, low-level media guests, which also means other security will be present."

Security Michael hadn't worked with before. He didn't look up from the papers contained within the plain folder. "I'll need back-up when it comes to the convention appearance and details about any other staff members working the con and which guests they've been assigned to."

"The convention has their guests listed, and we're waiting on responses from their people. As for the extra staff, it's a matter you'll have to persuade her about. Until now she's been adamant about this. One man or woman, no more. She doesn't want to make things uncomfortable for the others at the convention or be tripping over people at her house. Don't get me wrong. I agree with you. That particular event is a disaster waiting to happen if there aren't enough eyes on the situation and the threat is real."

Was there a chance the threat wasn't real? Of course, but a quick read-through of the file suggested she was correct. Something was going on. Likely a low-level stalking case. Still, Michael wasn't a fool, and he'd take more time to read through the information before he went to talk to the woman. Perhaps there was more here than an annoyance, and even a low-threat stalker could up the ante. It wouldn't be the first time a stalker had turned into a kidnapper or murderer.

Not this time.

"If she thinks attending this convention in safety can be done without backup, we'll have a problem." Michael scowled. It couldn't be done, not with the number of people that would be at the convention. It would be hard enough being the only member of security assigned to the woman when she was at home, but events? That was another matter entirely. How the hell was he supposed to manage things when she went to the restroom or when he needed a break? "Perhaps if I suggest we use Mags as a secondary." Yes, bringing in a woman might be better. "She'd blend in with this crowd, which might make her an easier sell to the client."

Shadows of the Past

Mags. A flicker of a smile twitched his lips before he brought it back under control. A good woman, talented, experienced, with a geeky side he had teased her about time and again. She'd fit in with the convention crowd far more than he would. Perhaps he could slip Mags in? He'd know more once he'd met the client. Unlike some of the other guys in the team, Mags gave off a nonthreatening vibe that would be important both to the client and at the convention.

God alone knew how he was going to fit in at the event. Shit, would she expect him to dress up and wear a costume?

Michael bit back a snort. Like that was ever going to happen.

"It's up to you to discuss with the client, but I agree Mags would be your best bet there, and I believe it wouldn't be her first time at a convention."

Michael closed the folder and frowned. Lots of small details. Things that might have been moved, a few packages and cards here and there, and a footprint outside of one window. A print too large to be the client's, but it didn't rule out a yard worker or a neighbor checking in on the woman. "And is the threat a real one? Or is this nothing more than the fears of a high-strung artistic type?" He tapped the folder. Unlike his ex, this woman was dark-haired, taller than Olivia from the details in the file, and younger by at least a year. "I know what it says here and what I'm picking up from a brief read-through, but I want your thoughts." *It's real, but how much of it remains to be seen. Some of this might be her imagination, or she's overplaying it, but there's something going on.*

"And you have experience when it comes to, as you call them, artistic types?"

"Yes." More experience than he ever wanted to remember. *Olivia.*

God, his Olivia. Had it already been eight years since the blonde, faelike, beautiful, and so very creative woman had walked into his life? How many nights had he sat and watched her work with her clay? Or scribble down poetry that tore at the soul when she later read it to him, though he'd had to push her to share her words?

Flighty, elegant, intelligent, and high strung. There'd been fights, tears, screamed words and the occasional thrown mug, yet at the time he hadn't cared. It had been worth it.

Right up until the moment when she had pushed too far.

The last thing he needed was to deal with yet another creative type caught up in their daydreams and art, yet this was the job he'd signed up for.

"Well then, Michael, you shouldn't have an issue keeping the client in line. As for a real threat, yes, I think so. My gut says there's something here, and the client, if anything, has downplayed the situation." Harvey shifted his weight, the leather of the chair squeaking as he moved, the noise enough to draw Michael's attention back to the older man. "However, if you're uncomfortable and want to withdraw from this assignment, I'll understand."

Michael flinched at the words. This wasn't his Olivia. Shit, Olivia had never truly been his to begin with. She'd belonged to her art, and at the end of the day, he had walked away, unable to give her all the time and energy she'd demanded. "I've never pulled out of a job before. What makes you think I would do so this time?"

* * * *

Lily Elliot took a deep breath and held it for a count of ten before she released it with a muttered curse in the direction of her manager. How the hell was she supposed to work like this? Did the damned man not understand how she worked? Her time was finite. Things like sleep were needed in order to survive, and it wasn't an optional extra. She'd tried for the last five years to get him to see she wasn't a machine who could jump from one project to the next without a break, yet here they were again, faced with the same situation.

I could explain it to him. Again.

Not that it would help. Daniel Walker was a good man, decent manager, agent, handler—whatever title he was using at the time— but he'd never understand what it was like to walk in her shoes. Hell, if you asked the man how long it took to put a piece together,

Shadows of the Past

he'd smile and mumble something about an hour or two before he blushed and sheepishly admitted he had no clue.

He could try. He's been with me long enough to learn. It's not like things are going to change anytime soon. Maybe one day he would come to accept that she couldn't snap her fingers and have a completed piece ready for a client.

"Still with me, Lily?"

Lily closed her eyes for a second before she turned in her chair and met Daniel's gaze. "Yes, a little frustrated, that's all. I'm going over everything you've lined up for me and wondering when, exactly, I get to sleep in the next couple of months." She offered him a smile in the hopes of taking the sting out of her words.

Daniel's pale-green eyes narrowed. "Now Lily, you know it's nothing like that. You're overreacting. You know you can do this; you've done it before."

Was that what he truly believed? She wanted to protest, to find a way to get him to understand, but he didn't give her a chance to argue.

"You can easily handle this. Hell, you could manage twice the workload and still have time to spare." Daniel gestured toward her art table, then to the Cintiq screen attached to a powerful computer—one Lily had paid to be custom built for her work. "Between the traditional art and your digital work, I've handled enough inquiries over the past few months to keep you busy for at least a year."

A year by his estimate. God alone knew what it would break down to in real terms. Tension built between her shoulder blades. She could protest, tell him to drop a few of the jobs, but then what? Her reputation would suffer because he'd already agreed to the work on her behalf.

And that was my first mistake, letting him pick and choose most of my commissions. There'd been a good reason, at the time. She'd been swamped with family matters, and the emails and inquiries had piled up. Daniel had stepped up as a friend to help her out. Before she'd realized it, he'd taken over.

No, that's not true. I knew what was happening; I was relieved to have the help and then didn't want to upset Daniel by telling him to back off. So, she'd tried the subtle suggestions instead.

It hadn't worked.

"You should be celebrating." Daniel took a step toward her and paused. "With all of this work, you'll be able to build up the nest egg you keep talking about. Not that you need it. The house is paid for, you have a decent bank account, and you're in a healthy position."

"Sure, I'm stable right now, if I don't get sick and I'm able to work for the rest of my life." He would never understand, but as an artist, you couldn't guarantee work. Nor could you plan on working until the end of your days. Which meant building up not just a short-term healthy bank account but funds to cover retirement, long-term illness, or care centers.

In other words, she had to plan for the reality of life, not only the here and now. "Celebrating? When would I get the chance?"

"I'll help you plan something when you're caught up," Daniel offered.

"If I ever had the time to celebrate, then I'd do so. But with all this work and who knows what else you have lined up, I doubt I will ever have a chance to even enjoy a simple meal with friends in the next year." Lily tried to explain. Add in her stalker, and who knew when she would be safe enough to step into a restaurant long enough to relax over a meal and a glass of wine? Maybe, if she were lucky, she would be able to persuade her new security to accompany her?

"You're overreacting again." Daniel rolled his eyes. "Look, I can't make you take time off, but we both know it would be a wise idea. A night away, take in a movie or something, catch up with old friends. It will rejuvenate you. We both know it will do you the world of good."

That was his idea of helping her plan a break? An hour or two with old friends? Didn't he realize most of her friends lived in other

Shadows of the Past

states and her main contact with them was via email or social media? No, of course not, and she needed more than a couple of hours off. More like a weekend, or better yet, a couple of weeks, but the work kept piling up. The problem was when you were a freelancer, you worked when you could because you never knew when the next commission would land in your inbox. "You don't get it, do you?"

"Of course I do. You're overreacting. Buck up, kid. You can handle this."

She bit back a sigh. "Daniel, I've asked you not to call me that."

"What? You know I think of you as a kid sister." He closed the gap between them and rested one hand on her left shoulder. "It's why I'm protective of you."

God, how she wanted to believe him, but her gut said otherwise. It was the same when he called her a girl as if she were nothing more than a child. It wasn't about helping the woman but keeping her under his wing, regardless of whether she wanted him to or not.

"I understand, Daniel, but it doesn't… I don't…" She struggled to find the right words, but it didn't work. No matter what she said to him, he'd continue to call her kid and overbook her. *Maybe it's time to find a new manager? One who doesn't think I'm a kid who still needs adult supervision.* Her gut tightened at the thought. Daniel had been a part of her life for years. Could she step away from him? Would she be able to work with someone else? Maybe she didn't need a manager anymore. She'd balanced that aspect of her life before Daniel had stepped into the mix; she could do it again. But only if she found the courage to say something to him.

"Is there anything wrong?"

This was it; she could tell him how she felt and then…then what? There'd be a fight? She'd lose a friend and a manager? God, she wasn't ready for that right now. Not with everything else going on. Lily shook her head and pasted a smile on her face. "It's nothing. Never mind."

A flicker of something had flashed across Daniel's features before it vanished. "Your new security should be here soon. Did you want me to be around for the meeting? I mean, he should know everyone in your life, right? That way he doesn't jump me by mistake."

The change of topic threw Lily for a moment. "Yes, I think it might be wise." She caught the inside of her bottom lip between her teeth. "You know I don't like this idea, having a stranger in my life like this." Security. What would the damned man do? Act as if she was royalty or a big celebrity in need of constant watching?

Whatever he planned, she'd find a way to live with it until the stalker was caught and dealt with.

"Lily, it's a necessity if you believe you're in danger—"

"Believe?" Lily stood, her jaw tight, fingers clenched. "I know I am. You know I am. You've seen what's been happening to me." She pulled free from his touch and stalked to the far side of the room. What was wrong with him? He'd been there from the start, seen the buildup of problems from the first postcard to the boxes and phone calls. Daniel had arrived only minutes after she'd discovered the rose and card on her car. What did he think—this was all a joke? That she was overreacting to the idea of a stranger pushing their way into her life? Lily shivered as she turned and glared at him. "You're the one who talked me into going to the police in the first place. You said I would need police reports to prove there was something going on."

Daniel leaned back against the desk Lily had walked away from. "Yes, I did, but it was to help calm you down. Come on, Lily; you freaked out about small things. It was call the cops or call a doctor. It's not like you're in danger. This is a guy with a crush. What harm could he cause you?"

Is that what Daniel honestly thinks of me? I'm a scared kid unable to think straight? Cold sweat beaded down the length of her spine, and she swallowed hard to bring her rolling stomach under control. "Small things? That's what you call it? What harm? God, you don't get it, do you? Women are killed by stalkers every day."

"All right, maybe some of them aren't small, but come on, Lily. You can't deny you overreacted."

"Is that what you call a stranger leaving packages on your client's doorstep, Mr. Walker?" The strong, masculine voice caught her off guard, and she turned, searching for the source. "Personally, I'd call it a security risk, even if the items were left with nothing but good intentions. A risk someone else could easily exploit to the detriment of Ms. Elliot's health."

Her breath caught in the back of her throat as her eyes locked with a pair of ice-blue eyes framed by long pale lashes. A small scar marred the stranger's features at the corner of his left eye, and as she took him in, she noticed the second scar under his chin. Lily's chest tightened, and heat rippled through her body as she looked away from his face and let it move down the length of his body. Tight, toned muscles without the bulk that came from too much time in the gym moved beneath his dress pants and pale blue shirt as he walked into the room with a predator's dangerous grace. For a moment, she let her gaze linger on his groin before she realized what she was doing. Only then did she push back her nerves and let her annoyance break through, her voice sharp as she forced herself to look at his face.

"Like what you see, Ms. Elliot?" A cold, wicked smile claimed his lips. "I don't mind if you take a second look if you need a little more inspiration."

Yes, she did like what she'd seen, even though every fiber of her being warned her not to get too close to the newcomer. Inspiration? What the hell did he think he was here for? Nude modeling? Maybe a gigolo? Fine. The ideas intrigued her, but damn it all, this was her home; she wasn't going to be intimidated. She lifted her chin and forced herself to stand tall despite her lack of natural height. She wasn't alone. If he was a danger to her, then Daniel would call the cops, but would they make it in time if this newcomer was the stalker? "Who the hell are you? And what are you doing in my home?"

His gaze moved from Lily to Daniel and back again, a mischievous smile flashing across his handsome features. "You didn't tell her I was coming?"

Daniel coughed and cleared his throat. "Of course I told her, but neither of us heard a knock or a bell. You do have a bell on the door, don't you, Lily?"

"Yes, of course I do." And locks, ones she'd taken to double-checking each night or whenever she was alone. "How did you get in?"

"The door wasn't locked." The stranger shrugged. "You need to be more careful about security, given the situation. Don't you think?"

"I always lock the door," Lily protested. Why in hell's name was she answering him instead of demanding his name again? Daniel obviously knew who the man was and once again was treating her as a child. *This has to stop. I can't go on allowing Daniel to do this to me.*

"Did you remember when Mr. Walker arrived?"

"He let himself in; he has a key." Realization struck hard and fast as anger flared into life. She turned to stare at Daniel and somehow managed to keep her voice calm. How could he have been so careless? "You left it unlocked?"

"I didn't think anything about it. After all, I'm right here. It's not as if anyone's going to attack you when there are witnesses, kid," Daniel explained, his jaw tight. "Do you believe I would put you at risk? You are completely safe with me."

"It's that sort of thinking that gets people killed, Mr. Walker."

Killed? Lily wrapped her arms around her body and shrank into herself. How could she be safe with everything going on? Was Daniel that naive? No, this wasn't about being naïve. It was about believing there was a problem to begin with.

"Mr. Parker, you're exaggerating the situation." Daniel rested a hand on Lily's shoulder. "And you're frightening her. She doesn't need the stress. Perhaps we should discuss this elsewhere, away

Shadows of the Past

from Lily. She has a lot of work to do, and I don't want her shaken to the point where she's unable to focus."

Is this the security guy? Parker? Who else could it be? At least she now had a name to go with the face. She twisted to look up at Daniel, her back tight, stomach in knots. Only now did Daniel's words sink in. Unable to focus? Discuss the matter elsewhere? She scrambled for the right words. "Daniel—"

"I've got this, Lily." He didn't even glance her way. "He's trying to scare you."

Stop it. Stop saying my name as if you were in control of me. Of the situation. Of everything. She struggled, wanting to find the right words, a way of getting through to Daniel without ruining what was left of their friendship, but her mind refused to cooperate.

"She should be frightened, if even half of what was in the file is correct." The newcomer's voice turned cold, his words clipped and businesslike. "Stress affecting her work would only be the beginning of the problems she's going to face if this continues. Between the unlocked door, packages, and reports of strangers on the property, there's more going on here than the overactive imagination of an artist." Contempt touched his words.

What the hell is wrong with being an artist? Did this guy have a problem with what she did? If so, why had he taken the job? Her hands clenched, and she forced her fingers to open. No, she wouldn't let this guy, whoever the fuck he was, treat her like shit. *But I'll let Daniel get away with doing it?* That was about to change, or it would as soon as she found the courage to stand up to someone she counted as a friend.

If I find the courage needed. Why does he continue to do this to me?.

"Come on; you're over exaggerating the entire situation. I know there have been a few incidents, and Lily believes she's at risk, but triggering a panic attack isn't the way to go about this. I'm sure we can talk about all of this later. In fact, it would be best for all. I don't want to distract Lily from her work," Daniel said.

And there it was again, the suggestion she was a flighty young thing unable to cope with the pressures of life. Despite all that had been going on, Daniel had taken on far too many contracts on her behalf. Which version of herself was the truth in Daniel's eyes? Was it that she was a feather-headed artist or a hard-working woman able to cope with anything the world threw at her?

"I see. You believe the situation isn't as bad as the file suggests?" The newcomer's ice-blue eyes narrowed. "Yet you're willing to contract security to do, what? Soothe nerves?"

"Well, she can't work if she doesn't believe she's safe, and I didn't contract your firm, not exactly. Lily decided she wanted the additional help," Daniel explained, his hand still on Lily's shoulder. "I don't think you understand what it's like for Lily. She needs to be calm to work. Between her commissions and her appearances, she can't afford to be distracted. It's business."

Not entirely true. Yes, Daniel had discussed it with her, and she'd signed the paperwork, but he'd then pushed her into hiring the firm. A good idea, he'd said, and Detective Richmond had agreed with him. That had been the final push for her. A cop, one she had grown to trust, had told her he couldn't help her the way she needed and couldn't protect her if the stalker increased his attentions.

Parker arched an eyebrow. "I see."

Daniel sighed. "I'm glad you understand. Shall we take this elsewhere then? Perhaps outside or the coffee shop two blocks away?"

"Mr. Walker, what I understand is that you believe she's not at risk and this entire thing is to calm the ragged nerves of a high-strung artist. Unfortunately, I disagree with you. The latest incident, two damaged tires, combined with the reports from a Detective Richmond, says there's something going on. Richmond believes there is a problem. From reports and information he was willing to share with my agency, I'd agree there is a situation. It might be one stalker or several, but there is an unwanted presence in Ms. Elliot's life. Whoever is behind this is smart enough to make most of the issues appear to be accidents or, in your words, the reactions of a 'high-strung artist,' except for the gifts. It doesn't fit the main profile." A small frown creased his brow. "That implies there's more than one stalker involved in the situation, either working together or separately. My gut instinct is they're not working together. It's unlikely stalkers will do that if they are both fixated on the same target. It's a conflict of interests, which would eventually cause a fight, a split between them. It could still be one person behind all of this, but if so, they're torn between two sets of desires."

"Two stalkers? Both focused on Lily? Now you're being ridiculous." Daniel snorted, his hand tightening on her shoulder. "You're going to give her nightmares."

Lily pressed one hand to her stomach even as she winced from the pressure of Daniel's fingers as they dug into her flesh. Cold tendrils of doubt and fear snaked through her guts. Daniel didn't believe it was that bad? Why had he pressed for her to talk to the police then? To make reports? Had it all been to smooth things over with her? No, whatever was going on, she'd had enough. With a low growl, she yanked free of Daniel's touch and rounded on the two men. "Will the both of you stop talking as if I'm not even here?"

"Lily, I can handle this. Mr. Parker, if you'd like to follow me, we can—"

"No." Lily struggled to keep her voice calm despite the tightness in her chest. Enough was enough. "Daniel, I think you should go. I need to sit down with Mr. Parker and discuss a few things with him."

"Now, kid. You don't need to stress yourself out with all of this." Daniel smiled, though it didn't reach his eyes.

"I've asked you not to call me kid, Daniel. Please, leave me with Mr. Parker." She forced herself to meet Daniel's gaze. "This is my home and my life. I signed the agreement with Mr. Parker's firm, and any discussions need to involve me." Daniel started to protest, but she cut him off. "Yes, you handle a lot of the business side of things, but this is personal, and I believe I'd feel better discussing this without you."

Chapter Two

Michael watched in silence as the stocky Daniel Walker, Lily's business manager, stammered and argued with Lily for several long minutes. Daniel finally gave up and walked out of the house, leaving Michael alone with the beautiful, faelike woman as she walked to the front door. If the soft click was anything to go by, Lily locked it before she returned to the room with a gentle flush now marking her cheeks. His gaze narrowed on his assignment. Hands clenched at her sides, back straight, shoulders stiff as she walked, her jeans taut against her long, lithe legs. *Odd, I wouldn't have thought she'd have the strength to order him out like that.* There was no denying what Michael had witnessed or the emotions that vibrated from Lily with each determined step. Not only had she told Walker to leave, but she'd also refused to back down when he'd protested.

Good, she'd need that strength to cope with the changes his presence would force into her life.

Would she fight him the same way? Maybe, but only on things that truly mattered to her, things that might impact her ability to work or her privacy, which meant they would go head to head at least several times a day. Well, no one ever said he wanted a dull life, and with this assignment, he'd be forced to think on his feet; in other words, standard operating procedure.

The young woman sighed, and he bit back a smile as he tracked her movements. A sensual sway touched Lily's hips as she walked; her long dark hair whispered across her back, a temptation he wanted to tangle his fingers into and use as a leash to bring her against his chest. Would her back arch? Her lips part? Would she move against him, or would she go still?

Warm, compliant, with a touch of fire?

The idea caught him off guard, and he scowled. *Oh hell no.* Michael shook off the idea of touching her, tasting her, or finding out exactly how she might react to him sexually. Sure, she was attrac-

Shadows of the Past

tive, but he knew better than to touch an assignment. Shit, bad enough Kyle had fallen into that trap, and God alone knew he didn't begrudge Kyle finding a woman he could be himself with, but it didn't mean he was about to make the same error. Especially not with a woman who reminded him far too much of someone else.

Olivia.

No, Oliva was long gone, removed from his life, never to walk back in. So why, in dealing with Lily Elliot, were his thoughts drawn back to those younger years with the high-strung creative who had ripped his heart to shreds? He'd had the same reaction in Harvey's office when they had been going through the file. Sure, both women were artists, and there was a surface resemblance, but the spirit Lily had shown, the determination that had forced Walker to back down, were not things Olivia had hinted at.

At least not around him. Tears, hysterics, those had been far more the norm when it had come to how Olivia dealt with situations. A pity. If Olivia had been this strong, able to stand up to people, perhaps things would have been different between them.

Focus on the job at hand. The past is the past; there's no going back.

"Well now, down to business. Do you have a first name, Mr. Parker?" Lily rolled out her shoulder, the one Daniel had touched before she looked around the room and settled into the high-backed leather chair in front of her workstation. "After all, you know mine, and I would like to be on a level footing with you."

A level footing? Perhaps level surface would be more fitting? Yes, Lily stretched out beneath him on the bed, her hands above her head, clasped in one of his as he worshiped her lips and throat before he made his way down to the sweet curves of her breasts.

His cock thickened, and he blinked.

Enough. She's attractive, but this isn't a bar or a club. Fuck, this isn't like me. I don't lust over women on the job. It's time to stop sizing her up before I turn into a drooling fool.

"Michael." He made no move to sit as he offered her his name.

He was all too aware his body needed time to come down from the images his mind provided. Did Daniel's touch make her uncomfortable or was it the situation? The way Daniel had treated Lily with a mix of ownership and protection, combined with all too obvious condescension, unsettled Michael. He didn't like the man or the way he acted, as if Lily was incapable of looking after herself.

Why hadn't Lily fired Daniel Walker?

Michael bit back a sigh. This was a relationship he would have to consider if he was to understand the situation.

"Michael. All right, well I..." Her words drifted off as she caught her bottom lip between her teeth. Her eyelids half closed, eyes losing their focus as she fell silent.

"You're not comfortable with having me in your house." *Get this all out in the open; it will make it easier to work with her. Damnit, I hope she doesn't make a habit of that with her lip.* All he wanted to do was kiss it, tug it into his mouth as he stole her breath, but it wasn't going to happen.

"No," she admitted. "Would you be comfortable with a stranger in your house?"

"I've done it before, though it took me time to get used to." Being shoved into barracks with twenty other men hadn't been quite the same thing, but she didn't need to know, not immediately at least. *Not ever. This is work, not someone I'm going to spill my past to. I need to get this under control before I end up making a mistake.* Michael kept his face a mask of businesslike calm as he continued, determined not to allow Lily to see anything but the professional security he'd been hired to be. Who was he trying to fool, himself or the client? "We work with this. I'm not here to make your life uncomfortable but make it easier, allow you a sense of peace, so you don't focus on the risks. It will take a little work, and there will be a few small compromises, but you'll be safe in my care."

She'd be safer within the confines of his arms.

No. Not happening, remember? Get a grip. You're better than this.

Shadows of the Past

"Meanwhile my life will be turned upside down in the name of protection." A small frown marred her otherwise perfect brow. "No, I understand. I'm not safe, not with everything that's happened. And before you ask, no I don't know who's behind all of this or why they've fixated on me, but it has to end before it escalates." A soft tremor ran through her body, and her breath hitched. She rubbed the palms of her hands down her thighs before she folded her arms beneath her T-shirt-covered breasts. "God, any woman who watches the news knows how these things can spiral out of control."

Interesting. She understands at least some of the risks that come with stalkers. Okay, maybe there was more to this woman than met the eye. She wasn't ruled by panic, not yet at least, but there was a hint of it just beneath the surface. It was time to ask the hard questions and hope she knew more than had been included in the report. "When do you think it all started? What was the first sign you can remember?"

She tipped her head to the left, lifting her gaze to meet his. "Can you sit, please? I'm going to get a crick in my neck if I keep looking up at you. Anyone ever tell you that you're annoyingly tall?" A smile twitched at her lips.

"Not recently." Michael grinned and settled down into the leather couch against the wall. At least she had a sense of humor, something she would need to see her through all of this. Damn it all if he wasn't beginning to like the woman. *It ends at like. I can admire her form, but no way in hell am I going to touch the fire. That's how you end up in the ICU with third-degree burns.* "And six-foot-four isn't tall."

"It is when you're sitting down and having to look up at someone." Lily leaned back in her chair, and the tension eased from her body. "I have my own questions. Like why did you agree to take this job on, Mr. Parker, when it's obvious you have a problem with my line of work?"

"If I have any real problems, you'll be the first to know. This is a job, like many others I've taken on. Once I agree to the work, I follow through, and while you're under my care, you will remain safe." He watched her, taking in every small movement, the way she shifted with her long fingers now interlaced in her lap. "Back to business, Ms. Elliot. If I'm to do my job, then I need to know, from you, when you first noticed a problem."

Lily sighed, and the muscles tightened across her shoulders. "About nine months ago— No, closer to ten now. Must have been August last year, toward the end of the month."

"What happened?" he asked. How much had she noticed? Would repeating it help to trigger memories that hadn't made it into the report?

Lily closed her eyes and pressed the tips of her slender fingers against her temples. "It was nothing. At least I believed so at first. I even tried to convince myself I imagined the entire thing, but I couldn't ignore what was happening. Not long term. Anyway, it was a small thing. I came home after a meeting with a client, and there was something out of place in my studio." Her voice was gentle, thoughtful as she replayed the events. "I wasn't sure I'd seen the damned thing, but it was there, or rather it wasn't. Even tried to tell myself I was seeing things."

"What had you seen?" He followed the movement, the way she now massaged her head. A headache, or was that a part of her thought process? Michael wanted to ask, but she wasn't comfortable with him, not yet at least.

"A sketch card, a small thing. It was a piece that hadn't worked out. Normally I'd have filed it away or thrown it out, but I'd been in a hurry and forgotten, and it had been half shoved under the tower." She gestured at the computer tower on her desk. "It wasn't there. I lifted the tower, checked under my desk, everywhere it might have ended up, but it was gone. I even retraced my steps and checked my purse and coat, in case I'd stuffed it in there. It had happened before when I'd been distracted or running short of time, but I couldn't find it."

An art card? It took him a moment to remember what one was.

Shadows of the Past

Not that it mattered, but it didn't stop his gaze from moving to the desk in search of more of the small cards. Perhaps Lily would share them with him? Olivia had never liked to share her work with him. "What happened next?"

"I started noticing a lot of small things. A glass moved, a pen out of place, a piece of paper with a quick sketch missing from the scraps folder. Things that were almost right, and small enough to be easily overlooked. I started keeping track of what I was doing, more so than before, and discussed it with Daniel." The chair creaked as she shifted her weight. "He laughed it off at first but then seemed to accept what was going on. I didn't know, until you walked in, that he doesn't think the danger is real." She glanced down at the floor, her hands tangled together as she twisted them. "God, why did he lie to me? I trust him…" Her words trailed off.

Trust or trusted? That was something Michael knew he'd have to find out later. If she had lost all trust in Daniel, then it was time to part ways. Which brought up another question: how long had her manager been lying to her? Or was he downplaying the situation to keep her calm? He didn't know the man at all, and the file had suggested Daniel had been the one to reach out to Harvey, but it had been Lily who had signed the contract. Michael swore under his breath. He'd need to talk to the man as soon as possible and find out exactly what was going on.

"Whose idea was it to bring in security?"

"Detective Richmond."

Michael nodded, his gaze never leaving Lily's face, though for a moment he was drawn to her full, sensual lips. What would they taste like? Michael forced the thought back and kept to the business at hand. What had they been talking about? Yes, the detective.

"His name is in the reports."

"He's a good man. I think, at first, he believed I was overreacting, but when the first of the cards arrived, he began to take things a little more seriously. He tried to convince his captain there was something to the case, but the man blew it off, said there were more important things to spend money on than the hysterical imaginings of a flighty girl. His words, not mine." Lily wrapped her arms around her body. The action pulled her T-shirt tight against the firm curves of her tempting breasts. "I hate being called a girl. I'm not a child. Haven't been for a long time."

No, she's not a child. God, those breasts of hers, they'd fit in my hands without a problem. Would she move for me, push into my touch, or pull back and play shy? His heart rate increased, and his cock thickened at the idea. He had to get this under control if he was going to be able to do his job.

"The card, that would be the one left on the car with a white rose?" he prodded, and tried not to stare at her erect nipples outlined by the taut material. *Job. Focus on the information she can provide.* Shit, it had been too long since he'd found a play partner; it had to be the reason he was allowing Lily to distract him. Of course, now that he thought it through, it made perfect sense. He was a red-blooded man who hadn't had a partner in some time; he was reacting to the presence of an attractive, sensual woman. Nothing more, nothing less. "Or was there another card?" He kept the conversation going. The more information he could collect, the easier it would be to protect her.

"Yes, that's when Richmond started to take things seriously, though it's obvious Daniel didn't. Damnit, I wish he'd been honest with me." She stood and paced away from the desk to a large window that looked out onto a backyard. "It was the rose that changed everything. Very few people know what white roses mean to me. I don't think even Daniel knew about it, yet this stranger knew."

Michael waited, watching her. Would she explain about the rose, or would he have to push? Either way, he'd need the details if he was going to have a chance of tracking down the person behind all of this.

"My father, it was something he started leaving me—the white rose, I mean—but he's been dead for fifteen years. No one's left me a white rose since then. Shit, if it had only been the rose, but the note…" The words trailed off as she turned back from the window and met his gaze. "My father used to tell me to keep dreaming. No matter what happened in my life, I was to keep on chasing my dreams."

Michael knew from the report that the same words had been written on the note. "Who would have known about it, other than you?" Telling a child to chase their dreams wasn't unheard of, and if it weren't for the rose, he'd have shrugged this off as something the stalker had come up with, but when he combined the two, it left questions he had no answers for.

At least not yet.

"Mom, maybe. He used to say it when he checked on me at night, or when he saw me drawing. I don't remember him saying it around Mom." Lily rubbed one hand up and down her other arm; her head ducked, gaze lowered.

He tensed. Every inch of him demanded he rise, pull her into his arms, and cradle her. To do something that would let her know she was safe around him, protected, that he would never let anyone hurt her again.

Where the hell did that come from? It was one thing to want to fuck the woman, another to want to protect her. *Hold on, protecting her is a part of my job.* That didn't make his desire to keep her safe any less real.

"You think the threat is real, don't you?" Lily moved away from the window, her steps silent, a soft, subtle grace to her movements. "You believe me?"

"Yes, I do." He didn't hesitate. "There are too many things adding up here, including the packages, though I still believe there's a good chance there's a second person involved. The gifts are tacky, but the card and rose less so." Odd; he would have viewed the rose as tacky if it hadn't been for the card, the quality of the paper involved, and the elegant cursive script. Someone had taken a lot of time and effort to find out the small, intimate details that might call to Lily, even if they had only succeeded in frightening her. "They could be from the same person, different mood swings, but I'm not going to rule out a second."

"Whoever is behind this has gone to great lengths to find out some very personal details about my past. I don't know where they would have found the information to begin with." Lily turned her attention away from Michael, her gaze fixed on the fenced-in back-yard. "That's what worries me the most—where they, he, whoever, got the information from and what else they might have shared with the stalker."

"Odds are it was the stalker who found out, perhaps from something your father left behind. Either way, I'll get to the bottom of it, but for now I think my next step should be to check the rest of the grounds. I'll start with your backyard; there's only one way in or out of there, isn't there?"

"Yes, the only access is via the house. It didn't use to be that way, but I had the fencing changed when I bought the place."

"Why?" He rose, watching her as he moved toward the doors that would lead out into the yard.

"I like my privacy. Access to the yard from a source I couldn't control was something I wasn't comfortable with. I had better fences put in and removed the gate in the process. It also gave me more room out here. People don't realize how much you lose with a gate, but I don't suppose it matters to most."

"No, I guess not." He rested one hand on the door handle and glanced at her. "Is there anything else you want to tell me before I check the yard?"

"Not that I can think of."

LILY LEANED AGAINST the doorframe as she watched Michael walk into the fenced-off backyard, and she bit back a sigh. How the hell was she supposed to deal with a man like this in her house, in her life, for who alone knew how long? Fine, she needed pro-tection, someone who could find out who was behind the stalking incidents, but this man?

What's wrong with him? He knows the job, understands what

Shadows of the Past

needs to be done, so why is he a problem?

Because her body throbbed when she made the mistake of looking at him, and her nipples hardened and rubbed against the inside of her bra even as her sex clenched; a sensual heat left a coating of need on her nether lips. The man was sex on legs, and that meant trouble. He was the hired help, security, not a date, a boyfriend, or even a one-night stand. Not that she'd ever indulged in such a thing except in her dreams. In truth, the only sexual partner she'd had over the past couple of years had been one she kept in her bedside drawer along with a supply of AA batteries.

Michael continued to walk through the yard along the length of the fence, though what he was searching for, she could only guess. The only way in or out of the yard was through the house, and yet he tapped the fence as he walked along the perimeter. Now and then he stopped and pushed at the wooden slats before he continued to check the yard. The way he moved drew her attention, the strength and grace of his steps, the small imperfections that only added to his character combined to make it difficult for her to look away.

A man like Michael would have no problems when it came to finding a bed partner. Perhaps he was already married or at least engaged. She hadn't spotted a ring, but not all men wore one. Had there been anything on him that suggested a woman in his life? His clothing appeared well tended, but that didn't indicate a partner, especially not if the man was ex-military.

It shouldn't matter to her if he was married, taken or whatever; he wasn't here to provide her with anything more than protection, which was why he continued to investigate the fencing surrounding the yard.

He wouldn't find anything, not this time. Only once since all of this had begun had Lily found something in the yard, and it had been a single footprint by a small, stunted rose bush. A footprint she'd snapped a picture of, but by the time Detective Richmond had arrived to investigate, the print had vanished.

Had Richmond believed her or had the detective been humoring her? She didn't want to think that about the man. Besides, his actions didn't speak of someone playing along with a hysterical woman. He'd at least listened to her and hadn't treated her like a kid the way Daniel did.

Daniel. The stalkers. Who else, what else would come to light? What about the people Daniel worked with? He'd built up the agency after he'd started to take care of her contracts and obligations. Did they take the matter seriously, or was it nothing more than a joke to them? She'd met a few of them, mostly the assistant, a slender middle-aged man who always acted politely around her. What was his name? Evan? Yes, that was it. Was Evan also laughing at the oversensitive artist? Did they talk about her foolishness at a coffee shop, a bar, a club?

She pressed one hand to her mouth as her stomach protested and cold sweat formed across her brow.

Betrayal, lies, mockery. What else would she discover?

Her stomach rolled again, and she fixed her gaze on a small tree at the far side of the yard and focused on her breathing. In through the nose and out through the mouth as she counted to ten before she dared look away from the tree.

Panic attack?

No, she hadn't suffered from one of those in years.

Lily blinked and took a step into the yard. At least it was a sunny day, the type she would normally enjoy, but the events of the past couple of months had driven away her desire to spend time in the sun with a sketch pad or a good book. She'd let the stalker take that pleasure away from her or taint it to the point where she couldn't relax in her own home.

"Has anyone been back here, apart from you, in the last few days?" Michael paused by a small lavender bush.

"No, I'm the only one who's ever back here." She frowned and stepped out into the sunlight.

"What about Mr. Walker?" Michael glanced over at her, his gaze narrowed, shoulders taut. "Would he have any reason to be out here?"

She paused, going over the events of the last handful of days. Had Daniel ever been in the yard? Once, maybe twice since she'd bought the house, no more. "Not without me. He hasn't been out here this year. He has a thing about bees."

"A thing? Explain." Michael arched an eyebrow but didn't move from the fence.

"Allergic. Carries an EpiPen with him." Fine, it was a lot more than a thing.

"Ah." Michael nodded and turned his attention back to the fence. "Then we have a problem, Ms. Elliot."

"Lily," she corrected him. "What type of problem?"

"A footprint that doesn't match the information you've given me." He gestured to the ground. "If you'd come here, I'll show you what I mean."

Her throat tightened, and a light film of sweat formed down the length of her spine. Lily made her way across the yard toward the waiting man. Her heart raced as she approached him, and she inhaled deeply, catching herself a moment after she did it, but it was too late. No aftershave, but there was something there, a musk, a natural scent that drew her closer.

"Footprints. The single pair here but deep. Either he jumped the fence, or your visitor is very large." He crouched down and waved one hand at the area.

Lily let her gaze move over the man before she followed his gaze down to the imprint in the dirt. A frown creased her brow. A pair of deep shoe impressions stood out clearly against the dark earth. "Oh..." She nibbled on her bottom lip as she shifted to her left and crouched next to Michael. "We had heavy rain about four days ago; that would have affected the prints, right?"

"Yes, it would have shifted the dirt, if nothing else softened the print, perhaps knocked leaves down into it, but there's nothing here that suggests the prints have been disturbed." Michael shifted his weight and touched the rich dark earth to the right and below the prints. "Mostly dry, and the color in the prints matches the color of the surrounding soil." He sighed, rose, and took a step back. "I'm not the world's best tracker, and I'm no CSI, but my best guess would be the prints are only a day or so old." He reached into his pocket and pulled out his phone. A moment later he was taking pictures.

"Wait, I've got something that will work better than a cell phone." Keeping busy helped Lily push past the knot of fear and anxiety that had settled in her stomach. She flashed a smile and turned to hurry back into the house. How could he think to collect clear photographs with a cell phone? Sure, some of them had semidecent cameras built into the design, but they had nothing on her toys. It didn't take long before she returned to Michael, holding the strap to her high-end digital camera. "You'll be able to get better shots with this, and I thought you might need this to be able to gauge size later." She held up a simple metal ruler.

"Nice." Michael nodded.

It didn't take long to set up for the shot and take the photos Michael wanted, but once he'd completed the task, he turned the camera over in his hands, inspecting it. "Expensive?"

"Yes, but worth it. I use it to take reference shots, especially if I'm working with models." Lily took the ruler and slipped it into her back pocket.

"Do I want to know how much?"

"Probably not, but you need the right tools for the job." She took the camera back and slung the strap over her shoulder. Lily settled the camera against her hip and met Michael's eyes. "I can give you the memory card or email the photos. There's nothing else currently on the card; either works for me."

Michael nodded once and gestured toward the lawn. "We need to talk."

Lily inclined her head and stepped away from the fence, her camera snug against her hip. "What's wrong?"

Shadows of the Past

Michael paused, his ice-blue gaze narrowed, brow furrowed. "I know this should have been discussed before the contract was signed, but it would have been only mentioned as a possibility. Now, with the evidence in the yard, I don't think I have a choice."

"I'm not sure what you're talking about." Her stomach knotted, and she wrapped her hands about the camera strap.

"I'm moving in."

"What?" Lily's breath caught in the back of her throat. "No, you can't." Even as she protested, Lily knew he'd made the right choice. "Damnit all, I don't want you here." The words were weak, even to her own ears.

"I know you don't, and if I thought you'd be safe without me moving in, then I'd head off to the hotel and check in with you tomorrow morning."

Lily met his gaze. "Then I suppose I'd better show you to the guest room."

Chapter Three

He leaned in, his gaze focused on the screen. What was the newcomer doing?

He glanced at the notes scattered across his desk before he looked up at the door that led into his office. A touch from his fingers turned the sound up. Lily and the newcomer were too far away from the cameras with their built-in microphones for him to know exactly what was said, but he caught enough to understand he had a problem.

The security guy would be moving in.

No. That hadn't been a part of the plan.

He snarled and pushed back from the desk, turning off the monitor and noise with a click of the mouse.

The security, what was his name? He glanced at the desk, letting his gaze move over the scattered paperwork. Michael Parker. He had a place to start his investigations. This Michael would be a problem but one he could control if Michael kept his hands off Lily.

The woman was his, would always be his, even if she refused to accept it right now. Michael Parker and the people he worked with wouldn't change that, nor would the police detective or anyone else who walked into her life. Lily Elliot was his to love, to protect, and to teach.

Noise from beyond the closed door caught his attention. Women's voices. Laughing, talking, exchanging plans for the weekend. The sort of thing he would do with Lily soon enough, once she turned to him to seek out his affection and care.

Yes, all he had to do was push Lily a little more, make her realize he was the only one who could care for her, then everything would work out. Lily would be safe with him, his love, his wife, his partner, and all she had to do was accept it, and her fears would come to an end.

* * * *

Shadows of the Past

Something was off. Michael knew the moment he began to crawl his way back from sleep. The sheets, pillows, a dozen small things nagged at him, and yet he couldn't put the pieces together. Not immediately at least, but he'd work it out soon enough. Odd. Normally when he woke up, he could function smoothly without being locked in the fog of sleep. This time, his mind and body both were reluctant to surrender their hold on the welcoming warmth offered by the soft bedding.

He inhaled deeply, his nostrils flaring as he took in a scent that wasn't a normal part of his bedroom. Tempting and seductive, the scent held him, offering flashes of images, sensual limbs wrapped around his body even though he knew he was alone in the bed.

Is this my room?

The bedding felt wrong. He'd already accepted that fact, but the scent added to his confusion. Soft, natural, and definitely female. No harsh chemical perfume, only the simple background of deodorant and shampoo mixed with something odd. Paint? Oil paint maybe?

Why would there be the smell of oil paint in the room?

Lily.

Understanding flashed through him. He was in Lily's spare bedroom. The lithe, elegant, beautiful young woman who offered him nothing but work and danger. A woman he couldn't get out of his mind, nor did he want to.

His cock throbbed at the mental image of the woman. It punched out against his boxers, causing them to tent as he rolled onto his back. The bed creaked beneath him, the mattress shifting to adjust to his weight, and reality hit him as he threw off the last of his sleep. There was no denying it; he was at Lily's house. The pretty young artist who had protested, only the night before, against the idea of having him in her house overnight. She'd backed down, eventually, and had become reasonable about the situation even if she didn't like it.

It was a job, but his body had other ideas.

Would it be wrong to enjoy Lily? Not in person, but as a fantasy?

Michael's right hand slipped beneath his boxers and wrapped around the base of his erection as he shifted the boxers down with his free hand. His cock throbbed within his grasp, and he bit back a shudder. Damnit all, he needed this. She'd never know. It wasn't as if he would tell her, as it wasn't the type of thing that would come up in conversation.

Do it, enjoy the moment. It's all you're going to have.

What would her touch feel like? God, he wanted to know, but all he had was his imagination and the few accidental touches they had shared. It was enough to build a fantasy. She had a gentle touch, delicate skin, and sensual lips. He groaned at the thought, his hips moving in time to the strokes from his hand. Her lips. What would they feel like wrapped around the head of his cock? Would she be determined or nervous?

Tender and nervous; yes, that fit what he knew of her so far.

He closed his eyes and let himself sink into the image, his mind filling in the blanks as he moved his hand up and down the length of his erection. He reached down with his free hand and cupped his sac; a low groan slipped from his lips as his back arched, and he played through the images. Her lips. Tongue. Teeth. Fingers.

The muscles in his thighs tightened, his heels pressed into the bed, and he thrust up into his hand, fucking into the mouth his imagination provided.

So good. Feels so fucking wonderful. He wanted this, needed this, needed her. Lily was his. In this moment, this fantasy, Lily was his. Her sweet lips wrapped around his cock, her tongue pressed against the underside of his erection, and she took him, full and deep into her throat and…

His cock throbbed once, twice, three times as his seed pumped free, coating his hand. He groaned, his teeth clenched, jaw tight, his back arched in that moment of release.

Michael's heart raced and tried to relax, letting the tension ease from his body, his cock no longer eager for attention though he

Shadows of the Past

understood his flesh would jump if tempted again. He sighed and flipped back the sheets, rolled out of bed, and stood up. The small bedroom had a connecting door to an even smaller bathroom with a sink, shower, and toilet.

What the hell was he doing, masturbating to his assignment? Shit, if any of the guys had mentioned doing the same thing, he'd have laughed at them, yet he'd done it. It wasn't professional.

If she never finds out, there isn't a problem.

A hot shower and clean clothes would put him on a better footing.

A quick glance at the clock told him it was already seven, and if Lily wasn't up, she soon would be. He reached in and turned on the water, letting his mind wander. The last artist he'd known had been a night owl, and Lily had still been working at eleven, though he was aware she had closed down her computer not long after that. He hadn't retired until he'd been certain the artist had gone to her room, but it hadn't meant she had gone to bed. There was a chance she'd sat up and rea or sketched for several hours, but he wouldn't know until he spoke with her this morning.

With a sigh, he stepped into the water.

Working with Lily would continue to be interesting and challenging.

* * * *

Lily wrapped her hands around the steaming cup of tea and stepped out into the backyard. Gentle, early-morning light filtered down through a thin covering of clouds, and she closed her eyes, taking a moment to listen to birdsong and the soft rustle of the spring leaves. The yellow heads of flowers bobbed next to red and orange ones, the first flowers of the year dancing together in the light breeze as it caressed its way across the garden. Spring flowers and the fresh air that came with new life. There was nothing quite so beautiful, at least not to Lily. Nature's art called to her on a regular basis. How many mornings had she sat out here with a sketchbook to begin the day?

Not as often since her workload had tripled, thanks to Daniel. Damn, she missed her stolen time, and there had to be a way of getting it back without causing a fight with her manager.

No, there isn't. I've tried, a dozen times and more, to get him to see sense, but he doesn't get it.

She shook off the thought and made her way to one of two lawn chairs beneath the cottonwood tree. Spending time out here hadn't been easy since the stalker had entered her life, but Lily had struggled to keep her life normal where she could. She glanced back at the door before curling up on the padded seat, her robe tucked around her legs, keeping them covered as she relaxed with her tea. A morning ritual, one she indulged in most days for a few minutes, though the time outside depended on the weather, something that could be hit or miss in Minnesota at any time of year. It wasn't unheard of for there to be a heavy snowfall as late as April, or random snowfalls could strike in May or even June. Such was life in the Midwest. Wait three minutes, and the weather would change.

"Morning." The male voice caught her off guard.

Lily twisted in the chair; one hand lifted to shade her eyes. "Did I wake you?" Had she made a lot of noise in the kitchen? She frowned and tried to remember what she'd done to cause him to wake up this early. Michael stood in the open doorway still wearing the same dress pants he'd worn the night before, though this time he had on a simple pocketed T-shirt instead of a shirt and tie. She glanced down to his feet and smiled. Bare. Not what she'd expected to see in a professional like Michael, but it fit him.

"No. I woke on my own. I'm an early riser. It's part of the job." He flashed a smile. "That coffee?"

"Tea, but there's coffee in the kitchen, middle cabinet, bottom shelf. It shouldn't take long to run a fresh pot." She didn't normally make a pot for herself, preferring tea unless she had guests. It was a waste, at least to her, to put on an entire pot for one person, especially when she rarely drank more than two cups of the stuff a day even when there was someone to share it with.

Shadows of the Past

Maybe I should invest in one of those one-cup things?

"Mind if I…" He gestured back at the kitchen.

"Go ahead; you need to get used to the layout if you're going to be here for any length of time." God alone knew she wasn't going to wait on him. She frowned at the idea as he disappeared back into the house. Did that make her selfish or lazy? Neither. He was here to work, not to be a houseguest, yet she couldn't help but feel guilty about not getting up to put the coffee on or see if there was anything else he needed.

Stop it; he's not expecting me to look after him.

Lily sat up on the edge of the seat and held the cup of tea, taking a sip from it as she tried to turn her attention back to the flowers. How often had the stalker been in the yard? Had he managed to get into her house as well? She glanced at the fence. Was it no longer safe out here? Her skin crawled, and she bit back a whimper. Fear led to panic, and regardless of what was going on, she wasn't going to give in to that. Besides, Michael was here, and his presence would reduce the chances of the stalker gaining access.

Had the photographs helped?

She'd handed him the SD card, and he'd emailed the images using a laptop he'd brought in.

Had Michael known he would have to stay the night, or was the bag something he kept on hand just in case? Asking him would answer her questions, but would he mind? There was only one way to find out.

"Coffee's on. Did you want any, or are you fine with your tea?" He wrinkled his nose at the final word.

"Not a fan of tea?"

"Not really." He shrugged and walked into the yard. "Always struck me as the old maid type of drink or the sort of thing you see on those old-fashioned British TV shows. You know, the ones with those fancy cakes on tiered trays?"

Lily's hands tightened on the mug as she tried not to give in to the urge to laugh. Tried and failed. A rebellious giggle escaped her lips as it bubbled out past the rim of the mug.

"Something funny?"

"I can't…" She paused and set the mug down, the laughter taking control. Lily shook her head and lifted one hand to tell him to give her a minute to get it under control, but all she could do was give in to the laughter and let it work its way through her system. "High tea. You're talking about high bloody tea." The British swear word slipped out before she realized how appropriate the choice was, and her giggles turned into full-blown laughter.

"You're mocking me." He sighed and shook his head as he walked toward her.

A man like Michael should have frightened her. The strength in his body, the way he walked, all spoke of a danger that was barely covered by the image of a civilized man. It only added to her now-hysterical giggles.

"Keep it up, and I'll have to spank you." His smile took the sting out of his words, and she met his gaze. Michael ducked his head. "Sorry, that wasn't exactly professional."

"Spank me? You're kidding, right?" She choked back the laughter even as a warm tingle worked its way through her body. He was fine; a little teasing never hurt anyone.

"Nope."

Lily blinked and swallowed hard. Would he do that to her? If so, how would he do it? Put her over his knee? Heat coated her inner walls at the image, and she squirmed as she tried to push the image to the back of her mind. Was he a playful type, or was this a part of who he was? Lily shifted her weight on the edge of the seat, her thighs pressed tightly together as she found herself unable to turn away from Michael. "Oh. That's, erm…interesting." Her cheeks burned.

"Is there something wrong?" Michael took a step toward her, his gaze intense, hands loose at his sides. "I know I was out of line with that remark."

"I'm fine, really." She shook her head but refused to say any-

Shadows of the Past

thing more. No, she wasn't about to discuss this with him. It was foolish. She didn't go in for those types of games. Sure, a lot of her art commissions fell into the kinky spectrum, but it didn't mean she had any personal experience. Nor had she had any interest in it.

Until now.

Her breasts tightened, nipples beading until they were hardened pebbles that pushed against her clothing. She wanted to look away, to do something other than be locked by Michael's gaze, but she couldn't move. Lily swiped the tip of her tongue over her bottom lip, and only the tremble of her hands told her this wasn't a dream.

"At least I got you to stop laughing at me." He nodded toward her tea. "You'd better drink it before it gets cold." He turned and walked back into the house without another word.

God, what had gotten into her? She glanced down at the tea and took a sip, giving herself a moment to catch her breath and her thoughts. The man was a menace. How did the security firm expect her to work with a man like Michael in her house?

Use him as inspiration.

Her lips twitched into a smile. Michael wouldn't be the first person she'd used as a source for her art, but under normal circumstances, she would have asked for permission. She watched the door. Michael might have an objection to being used as a muse or an art model, and his actions the day before had made it clear he had a problem with artists, even if he refused to explain why.

"So, what's on the list for today?" Michael stepped back out into the yard. Steam rose from the mug he held in one hand. "Business or a lazy day?" His gaze moved over her body.

A deep shiver ran through her, and her skin tingled beneath his gaze. God, did he know what he was doing to her? No, of course not. She doubted he even knew she existed as a woman. After all, she was nothing more than a job to him, right? He didn't want to be here, and no doubt he had a girlfriend waiting for him back home.

Hadn't he asked a question?

Yes, plans for the day. "I have a wine and art group this afternoon."

His features turned to stone. "That wasn't in the file."

"It's a new group, and I only signed up for it two days ago after the paperwork was finished for your boss." She gave a half shrug and turned her focus to her mostly empty mug. "Is there a problem?"

"No, it's just easier to plan when I know what's going on ahead of time." He took a step toward her.

Lily's skin tightened, her heart racing as she watched him. "Well, I could do this on my own, or you could sit in the car." *No, he has to be there. What if the stalker knows about the sip and paint? He might have signed up for the event.*

"I wouldn't be very good at my job if I let you walk in there without me, would I?" He leaned in and brushed one hand over her shoulder.

Lily jumped, eyes wide, nipples taut. Small electric shocks sparked dangerous paths through her body, connecting nipples and clit.

"I didn't mean to startle you." He paused, gaze locking with Lily's. "You had a little something on your sleeve."

"God, I'm sorry. I guess I'm a bit jumpy of late." *Hello, stalker in my life. I have every reason to be nervous.* Except that didn't fit with the way she was reacting around Michael. He wasn't a threat, except to keeping her panties dry, and she was going to have to get used to his presence in her life.

She had to get her reactions under control before he realized she was attracted to him.

"It's understandable." Michael turned his attention to the yard, releasing her. "Well, I'll finish this drink and then you can go over the plans for this event."

Lily shivered, her gaze following Michael. She had to keep this under control. It didn't matter that she was attracted to him; he wasn't here to be her boyfriend or even a one-night stand. The

Shadows of the Past

sooner she got her desires under control, the better it would be for both of them.

Chapter Four

"Harvey, this is ridiculous." Michael kept his voice pitched low as he paced down the drive toward his car, his cell phone pressed to his ear. This wasn't what he'd expected. Not only Lily but the situation. "There are other events that weren't in the file, and one of those is today."

"And the event is an issue?" Harvey's voice was clipped. A sign, at least to someone who knew the man, that Harvey was upset.

Michael unclenched his jaw and forced himself to keep his voice calm. Bad enough Harvey was angry at the situation, but the older man wasn't the one stuck out here trying to get things in order. "How the hell am I supposed to deal with this? I'm one man, and I've already had to move in here, which wasn't a part of the plan." No, the original idea had included Michael staying in a local hotel, which was where the rest of his clothing currently waited for him. "I'll need to swing by the hotel and grab my gear." Even though this was an instate job, he couldn't take half a day or longer to go home, and it wasn't the first time he'd had to live out of a suitcase. At least now he was close enough to Minneapolis to be able to pick up any-thing he needed during the assignment.

"Do you need to pull out of the job?" Harvey's voice returned to his standard cool business tone. "I can send someone else in, and we can assign you to another job."

Michael paused. The question struck hard and threatened to knock the wind out of him. Was he whining over nothing? Looking for reasons to walk away from the job? "No, it's fine, blowing off some steam here." Lily. What was it about the woman that got to him? Whatever it was, he wasn't about to abandon the assignment.

"Then there's no problem," Harvey confirmed.

"Did you get the email?"

"With the photographs, yes. I've got Mags and David going over them. Between the pair, they should be able to pull out all the in-

Shadows of the Past

formation we need from the shots. Good quality there, not from your phone."

"Ms. Elliot lent me her camera."

Harvey coughed, clearing his throat on the other end of the line. "I see. So you could say you're getting along with her, despite the hiccup about the extra event. After all, she wouldn't lend you her camera if she wasn't at least mostly comfortable with you."

God, Michael wanted to argue that one, but it made sense. Why couldn't he see this when it came to Lily? "Fair point. I'll get back into the swing of things and see if I can get Li— Ms. Elliot to be a little more considerate about informing me as to what's going on. This afternoon event is likely pretty small, and it should be easy enough to keep an eye on those who attend. I can always take a few discreet pictures as reference." He'd use his phone this time though. No need to ask for the use of her camera.

"Keep me up to date."

"Will do." Michael ended the call and slipped his cell into his pocket before he glanced down at his still-bare feet. Lily, the damned woman, had him off balance, and that moment of teasing hadn't helped. He should never have threatened her with a spanking, because now he couldn't get the image out of his mind. His cock twitched, eager to find a way out as his body ached for the touch of the woman he'd been assigned to protect. Would she fight if he pulled her over his lap?

He groaned and closed his eyes. The only thing that kept him from reaching down and cupping his cock was the fact he was in her driveway. Why the hell hadn't she pulled on some clothing this morning? It hadn't helped to find her out in the backyard in her nightclothes. Sure, she was covered up, but the soft robe tempted him, and it would have been all too easy to pull the robe aside and see what lay beneath.

This isn't going to help.

No, of course daydreaming about Lily wasn't going to do any good, but it didn't prevent his mind from filling in the details. Lily was a deliciously attractive young woman. One he wanted to sink his teeth into. Not only his teeth but his—

"You okay out here?" Lily's voice pulled him from his thoughts. "Do you need anything?"

Yes, you, naked in my arms. Michael forced the image to the back of his mind as he turned and smiled. Lily stood in the open door, her robe tied in place, hair loose around her shoulders.

"Yes, touching base with the boss. The new event caught me off guard, but everything is fine." *And you're good enough to eat.* The words echoed through his mind, and he fought to keep the desire from showing. "I'll be back in a few. I need to pull a few things out of the car." He waved in the direction of the end of the drive.

"Understood. I'm going to hit the shower, and then it's back to work for me." She smiled, her full lips drawing his attention.

Michael tensed but managed to nod. "Sounds like a plan." Lily. Naked. In the shower.

Of course she'd be naked. You don't shower with your clothes on. Get a grip.

This wasn't like him, and he had boiled it down to the fact he'd been too long without a partner or playmate. He shook his head and walked down toward his car. He had no idea what Lily liked when it came to sex, nor was he in a position where he should ever find out. One thing he did know, at least according to the file, was the fact that there wasn't someone currently in Lily's life, nor had there been for a while.

Why a woman like Lily didn't have a boyfriend was beyond him.

Maybe she doesn't want one right now?

And maybe he'd ask her when they became more comfortable with each other?

Yeah, right.

Michael chuckled and walked over to his car.

Something fluttered on the windshield, and he stopped, his gaze fixed on the piece of paper. A flyer? No, he didn't think so. The hairs on the back of his neck stood up, and he moved around

Shadows of the Past

the car, leaning in close enough to see the paper without touching it. Large block letters written in blood-red ink crinkled and danced with each new touch of a playful breeze.

SHE'S MINE.

Two words; enough to make a statement and nothing more.

Michael swore under his breath and reached for his keys. A moment later he had the car open and pulled out a small silver case. Forensics weren't his thing but calling the police out would be a waste of time. No, better to try and collect the evidence himself and hope the team could help put the pieces together. He flipped open the case and pulled on a pair of white latex gloves, grabbed a plastic ziplock bag, and returned to the piece of paper stuck on the windshield. It didn't take long to collect the message and slide it into the bag. Once he had it sealed, he returned to the case and slid the bag inside before he locked it.

Hand it over to the cops? No, better to send it on to Harvey. They'd be able to check for prints and tap the company's resources.

The stalker knew Michael was here, which meant he was watching the house a lot more closely than first assumed.

How was he doing it?

Michael did a slow visual check for any obvious sign of an observer.

Nothing. That, however, didn't mean he wasn't being watched right now. He sighed and looked down at the case. Whoever was behind the note might well be the same person who had left the footprints in the backyard, but there was something that didn't fit with the idea of a man, or woman, who would leave a note on the car of a stranger.

A woman?

The idea had merit, and Lily would be less likely to notice a woman hanging around. Unless she was interested in women?

God, hope not.

His jaw clenched. If Lily did prefer women over men, then at least his problems were solved. He'd be able to fight his impulses toward Lily by reminding himself Lily wasn't interested in him. Except that the way she watched him, the sensual way she parted her lips combined with the change in her breathing, suggested she found him physically appealing.

It didn't matter. Work was just that—work—and Lily would only be a part of his life for as long as he was assigned to her, which wouldn't be long if he had his way. All he had to do was find the person or persons behind the stalking incidents and turn them over to the police. Then he'd be free to return to his life away from the all too attractive young artist.

* * * *

Lily paused on the sidewalk, shifted the weight of the bag of art supplies for the sip-and-paint, and glanced over at the silent man who stood back and to the left of her. Michael hadn't said much to her since they'd walked back in from his car that morning, but she'd been grateful for the quiet as it had allowed her to get on with her work and pretend he wasn't there. It was impossible to ignore him entirely, but she'd done her best to shut him out as she'd prepared herself for the event. He'd checked on her during the day, but his presence had been unobtrusive, and Lily had spent the best part of the day in her studio working on her computer. The time had allowed her to finish two quick commissions and send off a prelim sketch for a more in-depth assignment.

All in all, it had been a good day.

"Something wrong?" Michael inquired.

"No, nothing. I'm going over a few things before I face the crowds. I'm not always comfortable in crowds. The whole judging thing." She nodded toward the entrance of the coffee shop. Even from here she could see it was busier than she had expected, and she rubbed the palm of her right hand down her jeans. *Get the nerves under control. No one here is going to cause a problem.* People. What was it about people that did this to her? Oh, put her in a small group, and she was fine, especially if they were fellow creatives—artists, writers, people who understood the often-solitary life that came with her line of work.

"Do you need anything else before we head in?" His strong, warm voice wrapped around her.

"I've got everything I need."

"You didn't bring much with you." Michael moved to her side.

"The rest will be in there either already set up or in the process." She nodded toward the door. "I don't handle these things on my own. Daniel's involved. In fact, he's the one who arranged this event after pitching me the idea." Sip and paint events were becoming popular around the country, and it hadn't been a hard sell. "Should be fun now I've got my nerves under control. At least with people who come out for this type of thing, I don't normally have to deal with anyone giving me the once-over judgment look."

"You have an odd idea of fun." He shifted his weight but made no move toward the coffee shop.

"And what would yours be?" She turned and met his gaze.

"Hmm, a few beers with friends and a game. Unless you want all the down and dirty details." He leaned in a fraction.

Heat flushed across her cheeks. "And if I did?" What the hell was she saying?

"I'd suggest we talk about it later, away from other ears. After all, I wouldn't want to share all my deepest, darkest sexual secrets with you where anyone could hear me, would I? It might put you off your game in there, make it so you're not able to think about the lesson. That wouldn't be good for your reputation, would it?"

Her throat tightened even as her body reacted to the words. Heat crawled across her skin and into the core of her being—a liquid, needful desire that had no place in her life, at least not at this moment when she had to face men and women she didn't know. She swallowed, trying to clear her throat and force her mouth to work. "I see." How she managed to force those two words out when all she wanted to do was lean in and press herself against the taut lines of his well-formed body was beyond her.

Stop it. He's not going to be in my life long enough to risk any-

thing sexual.

What was wrong with one-night stands or brief encounters? It wasn't as if other people didn't indulge in them.

Nothing at all wrong with such encounters, but it didn't mean she was going to make that mistake with this particular man. He couldn't, after all, guard her if he was distracted by sex, could he?

"Not interested, is that it?"

Oh God, how she wanted to be able to lie. She coughed and turned away from him, giving herself a moment to gather her thoughts. "It's not the type of conversation to have in the middle of the street. As you said, anyone could hear you, right?" She flashed a smile, then nodded toward the coffee shop. "I don't want to be late." She didn't wait for him to reply but took a step toward the door. "Coming?"

"Of course." His voice was calm once more. All signs of teasing vanished and the professional mask was back in place. "But not in the way I'd like to right now."

Lily almost choked and took a moment to take a cleansing breath. *Good, I'm back under control again. I don't need to deal with lust in the middle of a class.* The man was walking, talking sex, and she wasn't about to pretend otherwise. At least, not to herself.

A light bell rang out as they walked into the coffee shop, and Lily pasted on her professional I-know-what-I'm-doing smile as she looked around. A dozen stations had been set up by a tall man with dark curly hair and a golden tan. He glanced over as Lily walked in and smiled.

"Lily, it's wonderful to see you again."

Lily paused and glanced around. They weren't alone, but the one person who should have been here was blatantly missing. She scowled as she turned and double checked in case she'd missed him, but no, she'd been right the first time. "Daniel not here?"

The man's smile faltered, and he ducked his head for a moment before he met her gaze. "No, sorry. He asked if I'd take care of things instead. Did you two have a fight? He wasn't very happy this morning, and I've never seen him lose his temper like that before. He was only shouting; at least he didn't go whole hog with throwing things around, not like Daniel would ever do that. Would he? No, of course not." He took a step toward her and frowned as his gaze focused on Michael. "This must be the new bodyguard?"

"John, this is Michael Parker." She half turned toward Michael before she continued. "Michael, this is John Wash, Daniel's assistant." Had the discussion yesterday led to this? Not something she would have expected from Daniel.

"Assistant?" Michael closed the gap between them, his voice sharp and businesslike. "You weren't mentioned in the paperwork. How the fuck did that get missed? It's not like Harvey to overlook things."

Lily scowled and rubbed the back of her neck as she tried to put the pieces together. "Daniel was supposed to provide the details of who worked with him; it's what we agreed when I signed with Harvey. Daniel promised me he would provide all the required information. I don't always know who he has on staff or who else he's working with." What else had Daniel failed to provide information about? Obviously, the sip and paint event and now the details of who worked with him, but had there been other things? God, what was she paying the man to do?

Good questions, and one he needs to answer damn quick before this gets out of hand. If it hasn't already.

"All he said was you were his client and how long he'd been working with you. He made no mention of an assistant or any other members of his company. In fact, the papers suggested he was a lone wolf operation," Michael explained.

John sniffed, his top lip curled in disgust. "Doesn't surprise me. Daniel likes to take credit for everything and do as little of the work as possible. But I can fill in the blanks for you, Mr. Parker. Ask what you need to know, and I'll answer. There's nothing to hide here."

"Michael will do. There's no need to be formal." Michael offered a hand, and the two men exchanged a brief shake. "There's a problem or two with Mr. Walker?"

"I wouldn't have believed it until recently, but he's been acting off balance. Jumpy whenever I mention Lily. Hyperprotective one minute, dismissive the next. It's not like him, or I thought it wasn't."

"What do you think might have caused the change in behavior?" Michael pressed.

A question Lily now wanted answers to, but they weren't alone in the coffee shop. Several women and one man had already arrived, and they were milling around, waiting for the start of the class. Tension built between her shoulder blades. How much longer did they have before she had to start the class? Ten minutes, maybe fifteen? Not enough time to have that conversation and allow her to calm down so she could face the students. "Can we have this discussion later when there aren't as many people around?"

"Yes, yes, of course." John waved at the art stations. "I need to finish setting up, but I have your station prepared." His smile widened, and his dark eyes twinkled. "I don't think I've forgotten anything, and there's an order in with the barista for your favorite tea and a glass of ice water."

Relief washed over her. "Thank you, John. You're a life saver." She closed the gap between them and wrapped one arm around the man in a quick hug. At least she could rely on John to cover for Daniel's mistakes or lack of interest. John hesitated for a moment before he returned the hug, his strong arm enfolding her close against his chest, but the hug ended before it became uncomfortable.

"All right, I need to finish setting up." Lily hefted the bag and smiled at the two men. "Lots to do. Michael, make yourself comfortable. I doubt there'll be anything for you to do."

"Oh, I'm sure I'll find something to keep me occupied." Michael let his gaze move over the coffee shop before it returned to the station Lily would be using.

Lily stiffened as she followed his gaze. Had he been looking at the other women? They were certainly watching both him and

Shadows of the Past

John. Not that she could blame the women. Both men were easy on the eyes. One of the women took a step toward Michael and offered a shy smile, one he returned minus the shyness before he walked to the counter and ordered a drink. The woman followed and tried to strike up a conversation. Lily's hand clenched on the bag, and she forced herself to turn away.

Jealousy had no place in her life. Michael had been hired to protect her, and if he wanted to flirt with a woman in front of her, Lily had no grounds to protest. Unless it prevented him from doing his job, which she doubted. The man was more than capable of handling multiple things at once.

The class; focus on the work. Lily opened her bag and began to set up the other items she needed.

"Your water and tea, Lily." John set the two cups down, one clear, one cream colored. "How are things going with your— What do I call him? A guard?"

Lily fought the urge to turn back and stare at Michael. "Security? Protection? I'll be damned if I have another answer for you. It's odd. I'm not used to having other people in my house." She gave a slight shrug and reached for her brush case. "He seems like a decent sort. I'm not sure how long he's going to be with me, but I'm hoping we can get to the bottom of the problem fairly quickly." The sooner the better as far as she was concerned. Only, that would mean she would never see him again.

"Any idea who's behind all of this?" John set the paints out and tidied away an empty cup.

"No, and that's making it all the harder. I can't imagine why anyone would want to make my life this miserable."

A flicker of something unreadable flashed across John's dark eyes. He shifted to grab a roll of paper towels.

"Is that what's happening? I'm sorry. Daniel hasn't told me much about the situation beyond a few cards and gifts. It sounded like the usual fan-type thing. I assumed it was an admirer, but bringing in security means what?"

"Means I don't feel safe in my own home." She sighed and pushed a strand of hair back from her eyes. God, how was she supposed to explain what it was like to live in fear, especially to a man like John? She cast a quick glance at him, taking in his appearance. He was strong, well built, handsome, and could no doubt handle himself.

"If someone was walking around the outside of your house, you could call the cops and hold your own if need be if they broke in. They might be after your money, or even if they were insane and wanted to hurt you, it's not the same as the fears I live with right now." She nibbled on her bottom lip. "A woman lives with other fears when it comes to stalkers; we're more likely to be victims of rape and murder from a stalker once they realize we're not interested in them. Most stalkers, at least from what I've read, don't even have direct contact with their targets, but they believe there's a relationship between themselves and their obsession." Was she making any sense in how she was explaining it?

John listened closely, his eyes half closed, one hand still wrapped around the paper towels. "You believe you're at risk? In some sort of danger?"

Lily sighed and tried to keep calm. "You don't believe me, do you?"

"No, it's not that. I'm trying to understand." He smiled and set the roll down. "I've worked with you and Daniel for a long time now, and I know you're not the type to overreact. I'm trying to put the pieces together. You know how it goes. You've heard Sharon complain about my habits more than once."

Daniel would never understand, but at least there was one person in his office who did. She smiled for a moment. Yes, Sharon, John's wife, had been quite verbal about her husband's habit of digging into situations to better understand them.

"All right, it makes sense." Lily checked over her brushes before she continued. "Yes, I'm afraid the stalker is going to increase his interest in me, and that it could lead to rape, kidnap, death, or all

Shadows of the Past

of the above. A reasonable fear, considering how close he's been to my house." She nodded toward Michael. "He found footprints in my backyard yesterday, which is why he's now staying at the house."

John turned to watch Michael. "You don't want him there, do you? At your home, I mean?"

"No, I don't." *Liar, liar, pants on fire.* She focused her attention on the brushes. "I'd like things to return to normal, but as long as the stalker is out there, it's not going to happen." She wasn't going to be a statistic.

* * * *

Michael settled into place with his cup of coffee and let his gaze move slowly around the coffee shop. Men and women, mostly women, had filled up the space, their voices soft as they spoke. Fourteen stations had been set up for the sip-and-paint event, and more than one hopeful artist had come away from the counter with a glass of wine instead of coffee or tea.

The location offered wine and high-end beer but no spirits, and the clientele didn't lack for funds, if their clothing was anything to go by. Good shoes, well-tended nails, but not the expensive wear you might find among the Prada and red-sole-shoe set. Comfortable, maybe wealthy, but not millionaires. Upper-middle class for the most part. Body types varied from the painfully thin to overly padded for his taste and everything in between. Some knew each other; others were obvious strangers, going by body language.

His gaze returned to Lily and the tall, dark-haired man she'd introduced. John Wash. Calm, confident, and professional, yet he remained physically close to Lily, perhaps a little more than was needed at this moment. Maybe it came from a previous friendship between them, but he hadn't been important enough for Lily to mention him in her information.

That detail, the omission of it, sat ill with Michael, but it was something he'd have to follow up on with Daniel and Harvey.

Michael pulled out his phone and shot a text off to his boss. The older man wouldn't be happy Daniel and Lily both had forgotten to mention John even in passing. Was John the type who faded into the background, like a barista or server? Maybe so, but from the way John leaned in to Lily when they spoke, he obviously didn't believe he was a piece of the background.

Something to watch? Or is he merely taking care of one of the clients? Hard to tell at the first meeting, but Michael wasn't picking up anything dangerous about the guy. He wasn't the only one in the place who was watching Lily. The barista's gaze kept moving toward her, and one of the men taking part in the class also paid close attention to what was going on.

"Not taking part?" Tall, curves in all the right places, and dark hair with hints of red, the woman behind the voice drew Michael's attention, if only for a moment, away from Lily.

"No, sorry. Not my thing." He took another sip of his coffee.

"Not mine either, but my sister needed a lift, so here I am." She settled into the spare chair. "Not taken, is it?"

"No." Confident woman. You had to be to sit down next to a strange man and only then ask if the chair was free.

"A person of few words. Have to like that in a man." She leaned in; the low cut of her dark-blue top offered a generous view of her cleavage. "Perhaps we can find something to tempt you into conversation. I'm Jackie."

"Michael." He let his gaze slide over the woman, taking in her tempting curves, shoulder-length hair, and full lips. Dressed for sex and out on the hunt, or was this how she always dressed? He shifted in his chair enough to glance at Jackie's long legs and her high heels. "Your sister?"

"The mousy one over in the corner." Jackie flicked a red-tipped nail in the direction of a petite young woman in jeans and a T-shirt. "She's into all this artsy stuff. Delusions of becoming an artist. You know the type."

"Yes, I do." Michael smiled at Jackie. *Bad move. Focus on the job.* Sure, Jackie was attractive, but she wasn't who he was interested in.

Shadows of the Past

"You here with someone then? You keep looking over at the woman running this joke of a class."

"You could say that." Joke. Was that what Jackie believed? Michael watched Lily, the way she smiled and led the class, encouraging those who needed it. Her entire face lit up as she explained the next step. "You don't approve of this type of thing?"

"It's a waste of my time and my sister's money. Still, if it keeps her from whining every other minute for the next couple of days, then I can deal with it."

Lily moved away from her station and walked over to the sister, but Michael wasn't the only one watching Lily. John's gaze never left the artist as she moved through the coffee shop. John kept himself busy clearing scraps away from the stations, refilling waters, offering changes in brushes even as he watched Lily. His focus remained locked on the artist.

Not that Michael could blame him. Lily was beautiful; the way she walked drew the eye, the sensual roll of her hips called to him, and her soft voice wrapped around him, offering temptations he wanted to surrender to. John worked with her; his interest could easily be that of a man watching over a client or a friend. There was nothing in how John reacted to suggest he was sexually interested in Lily, but neither was there anything that said he wasn't. Right now, John fell into a neutral state where he could go either way.

A hand touched Michael's thigh, and he turned his attention back to Jackie.

"You're not into this scene, and they're going to be busy for some time. Why don't you and I go somewhere else and enjoy ourselves?"

His cock didn't even twitch. What the hell was wrong with him? The woman was attractive, willing, even aggressive, which could turn into an interesting time, and yet there was nothing. *Because I'm working?* No, he'd reacted to women when he'd been on the job before now, not that he'd ever stepped away from his work to enjoy an invitation, but he had exchanged numbers and taken them up on the offer when the time had been there.

Jackie slid her hand farther up the length of his leg. "We'd be back before they even knew we were gone. They won't miss us."

He smiled but removed her hand. "Thanks, but not today. I'm working." He nodded toward Lily. "She's my client, and it wouldn't be professional."

"Professional... Oh, you're a hired stud. Got it. Makes sense, though why she'd hire you to sit here is beyond me when there are so many other things she could do with you."

If he'd been taking a sip of his drink, Michael would have choked on it. "Hired stud?" He chuckled and kept his attention on Lily. "Nothing like that."

"Come on; there's nothing to be ashamed of. Maybe you're not working right now, and your time with her starts after this thing of hers? Means you're free to spend time with me." Jackie leaned in close; the side of her breast brushed against his arm. "I've never paid for it before. Might be kinky. I don't mind a little kink thrown into the mix if that's your specialty, though she doesn't appear the type."

Michael shifted in his seat to so he could watch both Lily and Jackie but didn't say a word.

"Come on, you know we can do this. I'll double your fee, if that's the issue. Surely it would ease any problems for you. I mean, about being professional." Jackie reached out and placed a hand on his leg again. She leaned forward, and her top parted a touch more. "She won't even miss you."

Did the woman not understand being turned down? Had he led her on? He frowned and pushed her hand away. "You're not used to being told no, are you?"

Jackie pouted, and a frown creased her brow. "You're turning me down?" She blinked and leaned back in her chair. "You'd turn me down for her?" She ran the tips of her fingers over the curves of her breasts, then gestured toward Lily. "There's almost nothing to her."

Shadows of the Past

That was not how Michael would have described Lily, but it wasn't the point. "Look, it's nothing personal. I'm working, she's my assignment, and I don't walk out on a job. Bad for business."

Jackie snorted, rose from her seat, and tossed her hair. "You don't know what you're missing out on, and now you never will. You won't get far in your line of work if you keep turning down clients. It's a fast way to end up fired by whichever firm you're working for."

Lily's soft voice, filled with encouragement for the woman she stood next to, drew his attention. Michael smiled, letting his gaze take in Lily, her grace and confidence as she guided Jackie's sister through the next step in the project. "Oh, I think I'll do just fine right where I am, Jackie."

LILY CLEANED ONE brush and changed to the next, her gaze half focused on the class. So far the event was progressing nicely. There were about a dozen students. Each one listened and followed her instructions as best as they could. There were a couple of real potentials in the group, the best being a young woman in T-shirt and jeans. Lily had only had to offer a couple of pieces of advice as they continued with the project, and the petite, shy, young hopeful had taken to the instructions with a joy and eagerness Lily understood all too well.

A few small encouragements, and the young artist had shone.

"You're a natural teacher," John murmured as she returned to her station. "You've never run one of these classes before, have you?"

"I'd never thought about it until recently," Lily admitted as she worked.

"You should do it more often; they love you out there. It's the same when you're at a convention; people flock to you, Lily. People love you." John settled into an empty chair nearby. "I've seen how you get people to respond to you. You don't treat them like they're strangers, only friends you've yet to discover."

She smiled at the idea. That fit her view on life, or how she had viewed it before the stalker had turned everything upside down. Now she wasn't sure, but in moments like this, she could all but forget about the chaos that had infected both her days and her dreams. Could she do more of these classes when the stalker was dealt with? Maybe set up a regular event here or somewhere else?

The idea appealed to her.

A soft sound caught her attention, and she looked around the busy room.

Michael had sat down at a table with a cup of something hot, but now he wasn't alone. Lily frowned as she took in the other occupant. Curvy, dripping sex appeal, and going by body language, she'd be all over Michael in a heartbeat if given a chance.

Bitch.

She tensed. When had she ever called another woman a bitch? It wasn't the type of thing she did. So why this time? Lily struggled to make sense of the reaction, but only one thing came to mind as a possible answer.

Michael.

Was she jealous? Even then, it wasn't the type of thing she'd normally say about another woman. Lily turned away as she led the class through the next step. She had no reason to be jealous. Michael had been hired to protect her. There was nothing personal between them, yet her stomach knotted and her hands clenched when she glanced over at the table.

"Is something wrong?" John leaned in, his gaze narrowed.

"Oh, no, nothing." She glanced over at Michael and the woman before she looked back at John. "Just a couple of things I'm working through. Stress. You understand?" She tried to smile, but it didn't work.

John scowled in the direction of Michael's table. "Isn't he supposed to be working, keeping an eye on you? Not flirting with the first available piece of ass who walks by?"

"Something like that." Lily nodded and turned her attention to the class. For the next five minutes, though it felt more like five hours, she led the class through the next stage. Only when she was certain the students had caught on to the instructions did she dare look over at the table again. The woman was still there, and she had a hand on Michael's leg!

Hussy.

Okay, that was more her style, but even then, it didn't fit her normal MO. Michael could flirt all he wanted, even allow another woman to touch him. Lily wasn't dating him, and there was nothing between them except a business arrangement that was temporary at best.

"He's not worth it, Lily. Don't let him get to you." John rested one hand on her shoulder and squeezed. "You've got a lot of friends, and worrying about a man like that..." His words trailed off, and he sighed. "You're not listening to me, are you?"

"I am. Believe me, I am." She inclined her head toward the table. "He's supposed to be working; it's the only reason why I'm upset about what's happening." Why else would she react like this? "Once the class is over and done with, I'll have a long chat with Mr. Parker about expected behavior while he's working for me."

"Perhaps request a replacement? A woman, maybe?"

"Sure, might be an idea." It made sense. If he couldn't keep it in his pants, then—

The woman at the table rose, spoke, and walked away, and Michael stayed where he was, his gaze fixed on Lily. It didn't make sense, not if he was so interested in the other woman that he allowed himself to be distracted by the stranger sitting at his table when he was supposed to be working. Why was Michael now looking at Lily?

Guilt?

Anything was possible.

"Maybe she had other things to do, but no doubt she passed him her number or more likely took his," John suggested.

"Not my concern." *Liar.*

"Good to hear. Wouldn't be wise to let a man like that worm his way into your heart."

"A man like that?" She turned enough to meet Michael's gaze.

"Lily, you only have to look at him to know what he's like. He's a player. Bet he breaks women's hearts all over the place. Besides, he's supposed to be focused on you, and yet he was there, flirting with someone else instead of doing his job." John kept his voice low and calm, his eyes half lidded as he reached for his drink. "I imagine he's the type women find attractive. I bet he's used to playing women at every chance he had."

Was that what Michael was like? Did he play around? How many women did he have on call? Cold sweat beaded across her breasts, and she looked away. It didn't matter; she wasn't involved with him. If he was involved with someone else, then it shouldn't be an issue. So why did the idea of him kissing, touching, making love to another woman upset her?

Whatever was going on between them, if there was anything at all, it had to wait until the class was over. Lily owed her students that much, and she was too much of a professional to let her own foolish concerns over a man she had no claim on take control of her life. With a newfound determination, she led the class through the rest of the event, only pausing to glance at Michael a dozen times.

By the time the class ended, Lily had come to realize what was going on. She'd accepted it even if she wasn't ready to embrace the idea yet. This was more than passing jealousy. What she experienced around Michael was foolish. It shouldn't have happened, especially not this quickly, yet she could no longer deny how she had reacted to Michael speaking with another woman.

A stranger touched the man who was supposed to watch over her.

A stranger drew his attention away from her.

But what right did Lily have to complain? She had no right to feel jealous or angry about the situation. They weren't dating, but Lily wanted Michael's hands on her, wanted to be the one trailing her hand up and down his thigh.

Shadows of the Past

Lily blinked back tears as she began to clean up her station. She knew she spoke to the students, complimented them, or gave them advice, but for the life of her, she had no clue what she said. The only thing she remained aware of was Michael's presence. He kept close, though he didn't speak and didn't interfere with what she was doing. Close enough to touch, yet it was something she didn't dare try. If she touched him, it would all be over. She'd do something foolish, and then what? He'd be forced to leave, to assign another person to protect her, and they'd never see each other again.

"Lily?" John brushed his fingers over her shoulder. "Can I get you anything? You're pale."

She shook her head. "I'm tired, and the stress of the past couple of weeks has gotten to me. I think I need a bath and an early night." A lie, but it was better than admitting the truth. She lifted her gaze long enough to meet Michael's before she turned away again. "It will pass, and life will return to normal."

John pulled her into an embrace, and she tensed.

"What you need is a good man. One who knows how to look after you and let you still be yourself." He released her from the hold and smiled. "He's out there, somewhere, waiting for you. All you have to do is open your eyes and find him."

Chapter Five

Michael Parker checked his rearview mirror and made the turn. So far there'd been nothing to suggest they were being followed, but it hadn't stopped him from being careful. All it took in situations like this was one foolish mistake. Cutting a corner once or twice could then lead to someone sliding in behind them and following them back to Lily's home. Not that the stalker needed to follow them to find out where she lived, but it didn't rule out other reasons for being followed.

They hadn't driven directly to the event but had stopped at Michael's hotel long enough for him to check out and pick up his suitcases. After the event was another matter entirely. They headed directly for her home, through the busy traffic, and out toward the small subdivision Lily called home. If there were any unusual cars in the area, it would be easy enough to spot them if he didn't allow himself to be distracted.

Like he almost had at the coffee shop.

Damn the woman. What had her name been? Oh yeah, Jackie. Why hadn't she taken the hint early on, and why hadn't he responded to her? She was his normal type. Not too skinny, enough to hold onto during a session. Obviously open to kink and very interested in him. He'd been without a partner long enough that he should have jumped at the chance with Jackie, and yet his body refused to show any level of interest in the woman.

Unlike the way he reacted to Lily.

He managed to hold back a groan as his cock throbbed and twitched beneath his pants.

Michael understood he had to get his reactions under control before Lily realized he was interested in her. Whatever was going on with him, he had to deal with it and get the stalker tracked down. Nothing else mattered at this point beyond her safety. Oddly, though, during the entire trip back to her home, Lily hadn't spoken.

Shadows of the Past

Sure, she'd been polite enough; she'd smiled and nodded toward him, but once the door had closed, she hadn't even looked his way. What was going on? Had he upset her? If so, what had he done?

Michael had barely turned the engine off before Lily opened the door, exited the car, and stalked her way to her house. A sharp slam warned him of a temper that was bubbling close to the surface. Fine. If she was upset with him, then she needed to tell him. If this was about someone else, again he needed to know, in case it had something to do with the stalker. It was all a matter of business.

Sure it is. Right.

Fine. He didn't like to see her hurt, and that was obviously what was going on, regardless of the cause.

He pulled his cases out of the back of the car and followed Lily into the house. Michael took a moment to go over what he knew. She'd been fine before the event, but afterward, things had gone downhill fast. Maybe she was reacting to the woman who had sat down at his table?

Maybe Lily assumed he wasn't doing his job? Anything was possible, and her reactions were far from outlandish for a woman dealing with a stalker. Fine. He'd screwed up by not being more forceful with Jackie, but he hadn't wanted to cause a scene at the coffee shop, which a fight with Jackie would have done.

"What are you doing in here?" Lily glanced back over her shoulder as he walked into her studio. Her hands rested on the keyboard, and she turned her attention back to the screen. "I have work to do."

"We need to talk."

"About?"

"What's wrong? What did I do to upset you?"

"What makes you say that?" Her tone remained cold, calm, and distant.

"The way you've been acting since we left the coffee shop." He walked toward her but stopped before he reached her chair. "When we got there, you were fine. We were talking, stopped by the hotel, went to the event. Since then, you've been cool, angry, and with-drawn."

"Have I? I wouldn't have thought you would have noticed. You seemed to be quite busy at the coffee shop with whatever her name was."

And there it was. Michael rubbed the back of his neck. "Her name was Jackie, and I told her I wasn't interested."

"When was that, after she grabbed your leg for the second time, or was that the first?" Lily turned in her chair and faced him, her eyes clouded with pain and confusion. "Not that it matters what you do with other women, but I don't think it's professional for you to flirt when you're supposed to be working."

He couldn't argue with that, except she was wrong when it came to one vital point. "I wasn't flirting with her. She was flirting with me."

Lily rose from her chair, her hands clenched at her sides. "You expect me to believe you?"

"Yes, I do. I've given you no reason to doubt me." He took a step toward her. "I'd never put you at risk. No more than I would anyone else I'd been assigned to protect." He was here to watch over her, to keep her safe as much as possible, and that didn't include him flirting with someone else. *But am I allowed to flirt with Lily?*

He wanted her. Had from the minute he'd walked into Lily's home. No, being honest, it had been that way before they'd met. The first time he'd seen her photo in the file, there'd been a pull he couldn't ignore no matter how hard he tried. Lily called to him. Her grace and odd mix of strength and fragility. She was everything he should keep away from, a woman who reminded him of his past, of-fered the same dangers with being an artist. Yet there were enough small differences that Michael understood he wanted her, not the memory. Not only her body, but her heart, her soul. He craved her, wanted to take her in his arms and kiss her senseless before he turned her over his knee and spanked her until she became soft and limp in his arms.

Shadows of the Past

"Just…just get out. I don't want to see you right now!" Lily shouted, her body racked with trembles. Twin spots of heat marked her cheeks, and her bottom lip quivered. "Please, leave. I can't do this right now. I need time to myself." She uncurled her hands and shook them out before they clenched again.

He should have walked out. Common sense said it was the wisest course of action, but his feet refused to move. "Why, Lily? Why does it matter to you if someone flirted with me?" He had a fair idea but needed to hear it from her lips.

Lily growled and looked away from him. "I don't like feeling like this. It doesn't make sense. You're here to work, to protect me, not anything else." She paced away from him and stopped, her back to him. "This is ridiculous. I'm sorry. I shouldn't be reacting like this. Give me some time to calm down and get my head straight, please."

"Talk to me."

Her shoulders shook, and she raised her hands to her face, the soft sound unmistakable. "Please, I can't. I don't like being humiliated."

He moved before he realized he was doing it. Every inch of his body screamed at him to hold Lily, calm her, and find a way to soothe her pain away. He wrapped his arms around her and pulled Lily against his chest. "I'd never purposely humiliate you, Lily. I'm into a lot of kinky things, but that isn't one of them. Please, talk to me. We can't move forward if you try to run away from me."

"Is that what I've done?" She didn't fight his hold.

"In some respects, yes."

"It doesn't look like that from my side of things, Michael. I wasn't running. I told you I needed to be left alone." A delicate tremble claimed her. "Please, this is wrong. You're supposed to be protecting me, not holding me."

"This is protecting you." His cock pressed against the inside of his pants. He wanted to do far more than this. Holding her felt right, but it was only the start of it. He could imagine her naked and willing in his arms, but would she ever allow him to touch her intimately? "Do I want to do more than hold you? Yes. I'm not going to lie. I can't explain it, and it's not something I should want. You're a client. It's not professional. Yet there it is."

She tensed at his words, her voice gentle. "I want more as well. It's why I was so angry about the woman in the coffee shop. God, I know it's stupid."

"No, it's not stupid. Do you know how I felt when you let that guy, John, hug you? I know he's a friend. You work with him, or he works for you, but God I wanted to yank him away from you and punch his damned lights out." He growled as his grip on Lily tightened. "I wanted to scream out that you're mine. That's what my heart says. My mind screams a warning when I look at you, but my body wants you. Like you, I'm fighting this entire situation. Lily, if you want me gone, I can leave. We can get someone else in to take my place. It would be safer, for both of us. I can't be objective right now." Michael knew this was a mistake. Harvey would have his head for this, and the guys would torment him, especially after the way he'd teased Kyle.

"How can I be yours? I've known you for a little over a day." She turned in his arms and pressed her hands against his chest. "This doesn't make sense. I laid claim to you in the same way. It must be the same with how I reacted when I saw Jackie touch you." Her breath hitched. "The sane part of my mind tells me I need to move away from you; I should break free and find something else to do. But I can't. It's stupid. Foolish. Everything that's going on tells me it would be safer to escape. The stalker, the work I need to do, Daniel… It's all too much, and yet I'm still here, still in your arms."

"What do you want to do?" He leaned in and slid one hand up the length of her back and into her hair. "Tell me, Lily."

She licked her lips, her back arched. "I want you. Need you."

Michael smiled and brought his lips down over hers. She gasped, the sound swallowed by his lips before her eyes closed and she surrendered to his kiss.

LILY'S HEART RACED under the caress of his lips. This wasn't

Shadows of the Past

happening; it couldn't be happening, and yet there was no denying the warmth of his kiss. She groaned and parted her lips under the gentle pressure of his tongue. Her eyes closed as she relaxed beneath his touch. Her breasts tightened, and heat rippled through her body as she arched into him. His tongue claimed her mouth as he stroked, teased, and tempted her. She reached up and wrapped her arms around his neck; her breasts pressed against his chest as she matched him stroke for stroke; her breath and his merged into one.

She ached, her body desperate for what he had to offer. How long had it been since she had trusted a man enough to allow him access to her body? Too long. Even now she wasn't sure this was the right thing to do, but it was the only thing that made sense to her.

Michael broke the kiss and pulled back on her hair so she could meet his eyes once she opened hers. "Are you sure this is what you want?"

Lily caught her bottom lip between her teeth and met his gaze. "Yes," she murmured as she released her hold on her lip. "I shouldn't—we shouldn't, I mean—but I don't care. It's the only thing that's felt right since this whole stalker thing began. The only thing except for my art."

His smile lit up his face. "Good, because I don't want to stop. I will if you tell me to. I won't ever force you, Lily, but you need to know something, need to understand. In bed, I'm the one in charge."

Lily bit back a whimper even as her body demanded she push him to stop talking and go back to kissing her. Not only kissing but so much more. "I understand, I think. You're a Dominant. Is that the right term?"

"God, you're an innocent in all of this." He smoothed his hand down from her hair until his hand lay against the small of her back.

"You think I'm a virgin?" She bit back a laugh.

"No, not a virgin exactly. I meant you're innocent of the type of relationships I prefer." Michael brushed a soft kiss across her lips. "You've never stepped foot into the realm of dominance and submission, have you? Not even a light spanking."

Heat flushed across her cheeks. "No." Would he back away now that he knew? The image of his touch, of a spank from his strong hands, sent a shiver of need through her body.

"Then we need to set the ground rules."

Ground rules? What was he talking about? All he needed to do was take her to the bedroom and get on with it. She pressed against him and rolled her hips. Perhaps a little teasing from her end would be enough to get him to drop the conversation.

"Stop that." He moved without warning, grabbing her arms. "We need to discuss this. I don't play with anyone without discussing the rules. It's part of who I am."

Lily pouted. "Why?" What had gotten into her? She'd never come on to a guy like this before. "We're both adults and—"

"And neither of us are mind readers. If something goes wrong, we need to know when to stop." He held her away from his body, his voice firm, eyes hard. "It's called a safe word. A word or phrase you wouldn't normally say during sex. If you say it, I stop. No matter how much I want to continue, I've always respected a safe word."

"Why wouldn't saying no have the same effect?"

"Because sometimes a submissive says no as part of the game."

"Oh." She pulled back, and he released his grip on her arms. "Saying no as a game? It sounds kinky." She chuckled as she realized what she'd just said.

"That's the point." He relaxed and gave her a long, slow look up and down the length of her body. "God, you don't know how hard it is for me to keep my hands to myself right now."

Lily understood. Her hands itched with the need to reach out and stroke her fingers down his chest. Lily shivered and took a deep breath. "No, I think I understand."

"In the clubs, we use the traffic-light system. Green is good, yellow is a check-in, and red is stop. Would you be comfortable using that system?"

Simple, easy to remember, and workable. "Yes, I can do it." If that was what he wanted, then she'd use his system. Though she couldn't ever believe she'd be pushed into a situation where she'd have to say red or even yellow. What was he going to do? At most he'd spank her, and they'd have sex.

What if I'm wrong?

"Having second thoughts?"

"No, nothing like that." She glanced away from him, but as she did, Lily caught sight of the outline of his erection, thick and hard against his pants. What would his cock feel like in her hand? She ran the tip of her tongue over her bottom lip. She'd never truly liked going down on a guy, but with Michael she'd be willing to try.

Michael held out his hand. "Your bedroom or mine?"

She slipped one hand into his and glanced around her studio. For one mad moment, she wondered, Why not here in his room? She mused over the idea. If it went wrong between them, better to have it happen in his bedroom than a room she had to use on a daily basis. "Yours."

Michael pulled her close, and his strong arms wrapped around her. Lily sighed at the touch of his lips against her neck. Soft, nibbling kisses sent shivers through her body. She pressed against him, her nipples tight as she wrapped one arm around his neck; her hips tipped as she rolled them against him. Doubts faded, and all that remained was a need only he could answer.

"Why do you feel so right in my arms?"

"Why does it matter?" she asked and tipped her head, allowing him better access to her neck. "It's what we both want."

"What we need," he corrected before he led them both out of the studio.

She didn't argue with him. In silence, her hand still in his, she let him lead her up the stairs to the guest room, which had become his for the duration of his stay. Holding hands. When was the last time she had allowed someone to hold her hand? It was a small touch of intimacy and claim of ownership she didn't allow.

With Michael, it felt right.

"Remember, no matter what, I'll stop if you give me the word." He turned to look at her, one hand tangled in his, the other pressed against her cheek. "You have nothing to fear from me."

NO, THIS WASN'T happening.

He stared at the screen of his laptop, his hands clenched into fists on either side of the keyboard. How could Lily do this to him? And with that arrogant piece of meat who pretended to be her security? Didn't she see what that guy was after?

No, she was too trusting. She saw the chance for both love and romance in this man, someone who had been in her life for a day, maybe a little longer, but she was too naive. This was the type of man who would get what he wanted and then move on. Lily would be left heartbroken and unable to see the one who truly loved her.

The bastard would ruin everything. All his plans, his dreams would be destroyed by Michael's actions. Lily would be so hurt she'd keep all men at arm's length for years to come. He couldn't allow it to happen.

Michael had to go before she lost her heart to him.

But how? The man was professional security. He would be on the watch for trouble; it was the reason he'd been brought into Lily's life.

He swore, anger burning in the pit of his stomach. There had to be a way to get rid of the damned man.

All Michael wanted was sex from Lily. No commitment, no relationship, no love. Michael would use his precious, gentle Lily.

He pushed away from the chair and paced across the room. He couldn't allow Michael to hurt Lily...

Except that left a way to get to Michael through Lily. After all, the man wouldn't be satisfied with only a single taste of his beautiful Lily. No, a man like Michael would be back again and again. Only when he was tired of Lily would it be over and done with. He could apologize to Lily once Michael was out of the way, but he could and

Shadows of the Past

would use her to get rid of Michael.

And in time, when he explained it all to his Lily, she would come to understand it was for her own good.

He smiled. Yes, she would even thank him. After all, Lily belonged to him.

Chapter Six

Michael stopped outside his bedroom door and turned to meet Lily's gaze. "This is your last chance to back out. Once we walk into the room, I'm in charge. I don't submit in the bedroom or anywhere else, for that matter. Are you comfortable now you know how I am?" He cupped her cheek. "We can back out, and I won't think any less of you." Asking a woman to submit, even in a small way, to someone she barely knew was a risk. It could easily backfire on him. Shit, this could cost him his job, his career, and his reputation, but damn it all if she wasn't worth the risk.

Lily leaned into his hand and turned her face to nuzzle his palm. Her soft tongue traced a line across his flesh, and he groaned.

"Lily, I need a verbal answer."

She lifted her lips away from his hand and looked up at him. "I'm ready for this, Michael. I don't know much about your world, but I'm ready to learn."

He closed his eyes to give himself a moment to make sure he had full control of his reactions. Lily had no idea how sweet those words were to him or what she was about to step into. "From this point on you refer to me as Sir, is that clear?"

"Yes, Sir."

They had begun. Michael smiled and opened his eyes before he slid one hand into her hair and fisted it around the sensual strands. Long, beautiful dark hair, ideal to use as a leash, but for now he would take her through this one small step at a time. She arched in his hold, her eyes wide, lips parted in a delicate *O*. God, he could take her here, in the hall, push her up against a wall and slide right into her, but it would do them both a disservice. This was a woman who was meant to be loved and led slowly into the darkness of his world, his tastes.

There would be no turning away from Lily once he had finished tasting her. Lily was the type of woman you kept, collared, and trea-

Shadows of the Past

sured until the end of your days. His girl— No, not girl, his woman. She didn't like being called a girl. He could respect that.

Get through this first.

Planning a collaring should be the last thing on his mind, but now the idea had surfaced, he couldn't shut it out. Lily, kneeling at his feet, her throat bare and waiting for his collar. Her face turned upward, eyes wide, lips soft and ready for his kiss.

"Sir?"

The nervous whisper forced his thoughts back into focus. He smiled and used his grip on Lily's hair to tip her head back before he claimed her lips in a full, deep kiss. Michael's tongue parted Lily's lips as he claimed, conquered, and seared her as their tongues dueled and she went loose in his grip. His cock hardened and throbbed beneath his pants, and he groaned into Lily's mouth before he broke the kiss. Whatever doubts or questions Michael had, they could wait until tomorrow. What mattered at this moment was making sure she didn't regret her choice.

Michael pushed open the door to his room, and with one hand still in her hair, he pulled Lily into the bedroom before letting go. "Strip, and remember I expect obedience."

Her eyes widened as she looked up at him; twin points of heat flushed her cheeks as she took a step back. "You're still dressed... Sir."

"That's one."

Confusion flickered across her features. "I don't understand, Sir."

"You were told I expected obedience, and that's two."

Her fingers flew to the hem of her T-shirt, and she tugged it up over her head. "May I ask two what, Sir?"

His gaze moved to her bra-covered breasts. Not large, but a good handful with ripe nipples that poked against the cups of her bra. "Spanks for disobedience."

Lily paled and covered her chest with her hands.

"Do you want to add more, Lily, or use one of your words?"

Michael pressed. It wasn't going to be easy for her to accept his dominance, but he had to know she could follow through. Force wasn't something he was into, except in a mutually agreed game, and if she wanted to back out, he would let her without hesitation. "The choice is yours, Lily."

Lily lifted her gaze and lowered it again before she dropped her hands away from her breasts. "No, I can do this, Sir."

Can you, my Lily? God, he hoped so. He wanted to believe he would have the strength to let her walk away, but at this point he couldn't be certain. *Yes, of course I can.* He'd never hurt her, not like that. He loved her too much.

Love?

Fuck, he was screwed.

Lily hooked her fingers into the sides of her jeans after undoing the fly and eased them down her legs before she stepped out. Only then did he realize she'd already lost her shoes. Had she taken them off before she'd walked into her studio?

Yes, it was a habit of hers, bare or stocking feet in there, no outside footwear.

"Good, you can do this." He nodded his encouragement.

A small smile tugged at her lips as she reached behind her back for the clasp of her bra. With shy eyes, she met his gaze and un-hooked her bra. Lily drew her arms forward to hold the cloth in place for a few moments before she lowered her hands and dropped her bra onto the pile with her jeans and t-shirt.

It took every ounce of his self-control not to step forward and wrap her in his arms. A flush covered her breasts, and her uncertain gaze called to the darkness that lived within him. A darkness he knew many a Dominant struggled with, yet never had he faced it in the way he did now. He swallowed hard and held still as Lily reached for the sides of her panties and eased them down.

His gaze moved down her body to her now-uncovered mound. Dark hair, neatly trimmed, covered her sex, and she refrained from hiding her body with her hands, something many a new submissive attempted the first time they stripped for their Dominant. "Very nice. I won't put you through an inspection, Lily. Though that's a commonplace thing for a Dominant to do with a new submissive." God knew he didn't think he could prevent himself from going too far if he walked her through a full inspection.

"Thank you, Sir." Her voice was uncertain and shaky.

Michael walked over to the bed and sat on the edge. "Come here." He gestured to Lily and then to his lap. "First, you take your spanking." Two swats. It was hardly worth the effort, yet it would be a mistake to let the infringement slide.

Lily licked her bottom lip and nodded once before she took a step. A subtle quiver ran through her body as she moved, her arms loose at her sides, but her nerves were obvious. Despite it all, she obeyed him and moved to his right-hand side when he confirmed, with a curt gesture, where he wanted her to stand. Lily stood there until he tugged her down over his lap before he rested his left hand against his back and his right on the swell of her tight ass. She shivered beneath his touch as he trailed his fingertips across the taut curves.

"Discipline is a part of how I live. When I have a submissive, she is bound by my rules, and infractions or breaking those agreed rules will result in correction." He skimmed the palm of his hand over her backside. "You disobeyed my rule twice, and that means two spanks. Are you ready, Lily?"

"Yes, Sir," she whispered.

"Good." He lifted his hand before he brought it down with a loud crack against her upturned ass.

Lily jerked as a pain-filled gasp spilled from her lips.

He rubbed the red mark left behind by his hand. "A spanking for discipline is different from a spanking for pleasure, as I'm sure you'll find out in time." He worked the heat into her flesh until he felt Lily relax beneath his touch, and only then did he deliver the second spank. This time her cry was softer, the jerk of her limbs little more than a ripple of shock working its way through her body. "Two spanks and done, my Lily." He rubbed the new mark until it faded.

Lily shuddered but didn't move from her position across his lap until Michael helped her up and rose to stand in front of her. Without warning he reached for her, tangling his hands in Lily's hair before he claimed her lips. She gasped, arching into the kiss until her breathing became ragged and her knees weak, his hands the only thing keeping her in place.

Sweet wine, that was what her lips tasted like: pure bliss. And her low, needful moans filled the air as he pushed her back on the bed. It didn't matter that he was still dressed. Right now he needed to feel her stretched out beneath him. He pressed between her spread thighs, his cock thick and aching beneath his pants as he rolled his hips against her core. She arched, hips lifted, eyes half closed as she smoothed her hands over his back. He broke the kiss and trailed his lips down over her neck. He tasted, licked, and nibbled his way to her breasts before he captured one ripe nipple between his lips. She groaned; her hands tangled in his hair as she moved beneath the play of his teeth and tongue. Each flick of his tongue brought a new soft noise from her lips and a roll of her pelvis.

He wanted to draw this out, but he didn't know how long he could control his desire to take her. That was one of the reasons he'd kept his clothes on this long, but now they were too tight against his skin. Michael eased away from her and moved onto his knees. "Don't move."

Lily opened her eyes and watched him. "Yes, Sir." Her voice was ragged and breathy.

Michael smiled as he stared down at Lily and reached for his shirt. With deliberate slowness, he popped the buttons and opened the shirt before he tugged it free from his chest and tossed it to one side. He reached into his back pocket and pulled out his wallet, setting it on the bedside cabinet before he stripped out of his pants, socks, and boxers.

"I need you," Lily whispered.

Shadows of the Past

"Hands above your head, crossed at the wrist." He kept his voice calm despite the way his cock ached to fill her.

"Yes, Sir." She lifted her hands and set them above her head, crossed at the wrists.

"Don't move, and you do not have permission to come, my Lily."

A small frown flickered across her brow. "Yes, Sir."

For someone who had never dabbled in submission, Lily was handling the entire situation beautifully. With a smile, he eased down the length of her body, kissing and nibbling a path to her belly button. He swirled his tongue around the small indentation before he continued his path to the top of her mound. She groaned beneath his touch, trembles claiming her flesh as she struggled to hold position.

"So beautiful." His breath touched her dark curls.

A whimper of denial slipped from her lips.

Oh, he wanted to spank her for that. How could she not see she was beautiful? The denial was hard to miss, and it was something he would work with her on. Lily was beautiful and talented. Did she also doubt her skills? It hadn't appeared that way when she had been leading the class. No matter what she believed, he would teach Lily how the world saw her. No, not the world—how *he* saw her. The world itself didn't matter; he had to find a way to encourage Lily to accept how he saw her. All the beauty and strength that was so obvious to him.

He parted her thighs and blew gently over her sex, and she shivered.

With a gentle touch, he eased the dark pink lips sex apart and leaned in. He gave one long slow lick, tasting her. She moaned; her hips lifted into his touch, and he licked again. Each new swipe of his tongue teased a new sensual sound from Lily and urged him on. He circled her clit, trapped it between his lips, and sucked. With his eyes closed, he pleasured her until she shuddered beneath him, her struggle for control obvious, and he lifted his head away.

"Remember my order. Don't come, Lily."

"Yes, Sir," she gasped.

She was close, too close to push her any further right now. If he'd had her for a few days, Michael might have been able to back off, give her a few moments and start again and again until she begged, pleaded for him to let her finish. That would be too much right now. He didn't know how good her control was or how she would react to repeated denial. Some women took to it; others found it painful and not in a good way.

God, how he wanted to teach her everything he knew and pull her into his world full force, but it would only send her running for the hills. Baby steps. It was the only way it would work. He didn't have the patience this time to sit and wait before he took her, not when he was this ready, when his balls were so tight he could barely breathe, and all he wanted to do was slide between her thighs and claim her once and for all.

He lifted from between Lily's thighs and reached for his wallet. With a rip of foil, he opened the condom and slid it into place.

"You can tell me to stop anytime you want, my Lily." His. She would always be his. There was no going back from this, not with how he felt.

"Green." She whispered the word.

Michael smiled and eased between her legs; the head of his covered cock nudged at her swollen folds, and he waited until she met his gaze. Only then did he slide into her body. Tight wet heat clenched around his erection. Her inner walls rippled in welcome as he claimed her, and Michael leaned down and wrapped one hand around her wrists. Yes, this was what he had been waiting for. Her body beneath his, ready, able, and willing to please him.

"Mine."

Her eyes widened as a moment of fear flickered within them before she nodded. "Yours."

She'd forgotten the *Sir* twice now, but he'd deal with the infractions later. His body took over as he pushed into her and she rocked beneath him. Her low gasps urged him on even as she lifted her

Shadows of the Past

legs and locked them around his waist, her heels pressed against his buttocks.

"Yes, that's it, move with me." Michael didn't release his grip on her wrists as the pressure of her heels increased. Was she trying to take control? If so, he didn't believe it was a conscious decision. Slick sounds filled the air and merged with her gasps and his groans. His cock throbbed; pressure built with each new claiming of her body. He lost the ability to think as he claimed her. His balls slapped against her swollen sex as he moved faster with each new rock of his hips.

"Need to…" she whimpered.

"Wait, just wait." He was close, so very close.

"Please, Sir." Her sex clenched.

It was all he needed to hear. He arched; his hips pumped as Lily moved and writhed beneath him.

"Come for me; come for me now," he commanded as he let go of his control. His cock pulsed, his seed pushed from his body as he moved within her. Her inner walls tightened as her orgasm rippled through her core, and all he could think about was the fact that he was home.

For the first time in his life, he was truly home.

* * * *

Lily sighed and snuggled into the warm body at her side. One strong arm was flung over her waist, and she could feel each soft breath Michael took. How long they'd both been asleep before she'd finally woken was beyond her. Oh, she could have moved, lifted her head, and looked at the small alarm clock on the side table, but the thought of disturbing him sat ill with her.

Had they done the right thing?

Her body said yes, as did her heart, but her mind now questioned the decision. They didn't know each other. Michael had been hired to protect her, and he had to keep a distance between them. Yet they'd tumbled into bed as if there was nothing to stop them.

And she wanted to repeat their shared passion, not just once but a dozen times over. Her body readied itself; heat formed between her thighs, and her breath caught in the back of her throat. No, she needed time to think and talk with him. Yes, it had been wonderful, but where did they go from here?

Repeat session?

She squirmed at the idea and stilled, worried she might have woken Michael.

Would that be such a bad thing?

No, she wasn't going there. Not when she still needed time to work through what had happened.

Lily's stomach growled, and she risked turning enough to check the clock. If she didn't get herself up and moving soon, she'd never complete her work for the day, but the idea of leaving the safety of the warm bed and the strong arms wrapped around her waist didn't appeal to her.

"Stay with me." Michael tightened his grip and pulled her back against his chest.

God, she wanted to stay. "I can't. I need to get something to eat and finish my work for the day." Still, she snuggled in and sighed.

"Regretting what we did?" He nibbled the back of her neck, and she shivered.

"No, maybe..." She paused, giving herself a moment to think. "No, I don't regret it. There are a few things I need to work out, but what we did, it felt right." It had felt more than right, but she wasn't about to fill him in on all the details. Not yet at least. "You're the first man I've taken to my bed in several years."

He shifted behind her and cupped her breast with one hand. "Was it worth the wait?" He tweaked a trapped nipple.

Lily gasped as her hips rolled. "Yes." God, of course, she wanted more, but she hadn't lied to him. With a strength of will she hadn't known she possessed, Lily moved his hand away from her breast and eased out of bed. "I have to get some things done. Please, don't take this the wrong way, but if I don't keep on top of the work, I'll be struggling to catch up with the rest of the week, and we won't

Shadows of the Past

have time to redo this." Where were her clothes? She scowled and scanned the floor before she spotted them.

"Hmm, at least you want there to be a second time, though I should spank your ass for breaking the rules."

Lily glanced back over her shoulder and smiled. "I know, I'm still in the bedroom, and I'm supposed to call you Sir, right? Well, that was during sex or leading up to it, wasn't it?" Did he think she'd act all submissive when she had work to do?

"No, for last night. You forgot to call me Sir at least twice." He shrugged, a warm smile on his face. "But you're new to all of this, and the moment has passed, so it would be wrong to push things with you."

Lily rose and gathered her clothes. She'd need a shower before she went back to work, and there was no point in getting dressed to walk through her own home. It wasn't as if he hadn't already seen her naked, and yet her skin heated from a blush that claimed her body.

"Thank you. There has to be a line between my work and anything else." A relationship? Was that what they had? He'd already made it clear he wanted this to be more than a one-time thing.

"That's something I can and will respect." The bed creaked behind her.

"I need to get a shower before I grab a bite to eat, and no, you're not joining me." She cut the idea off before he had a chance to speak.

"Spoilsport." Michael laughed. "Fine, fine. Yes, I'd have joined you in the shower and distracted you for a short time."

At least he was honest. "I'll be downstairs in about fifteen minutes." She didn't wait for his response as she left the bedroom and headed for the shower. It didn't take long before she stepped into the hot stream of water and closed her eyes. Whatever plans he had for after the shower, she now knew he would respect her work and the time she required to get caught up with her assignments.

Had her last boyfriend respected her time in the same way?

Come to think of it, had any man in her life done so? Daniel certainly didn't, but this man, one who was all but a stranger, didn't need it explained to him in depth. No, he accepted her words and let her get on with her life.

Maybe things would change when he realized she really did need the time? It was one thing to give her the space and time for a day or so, another to do it long term. He could be playing her, but she doubted it. Not with the teasing way he had admitted to the shower plans and the good-natured acceptance of the line she'd drawn.

Fifteen minutes later, she was dressed in a pair of sweats, sports bra, and old T-shirt with her feet stuffed into a pair of deck shoes. Lily braided her hair into a single tail that sat in a damp rope down her back as she jogged down the stairs. Food. She needed tea and something to eat before she tackled the commissions. God alone knew how much more had backed up during her time with Michael, but she didn't regret her choice.

MICHAEL LISTENED TO the shower down the hallway and smiled. Lily, his sweet Lily. She would be his soon enough, once he managed to convince her she belonged to him. Fine, he'd come to terms with the fact that this wasn't a one-time thing. He'd known that before they'd entered his bedroom, but now he had to deal with the fallout. Lily was still his assignment, and he would continue to watch over her and protect her as best as he could. The trouble was, if the stalker was around, she'd be in danger.

Harvey.

Michael needed to call Harvey and see if they had any leads from the shoe impression. It was a long shot, but anything was worth considering at this point. If nothing else, the team might have been able to identify the size and make of the shoe. With those details, Michael knew he could reach out to the police and add to their file.

His stomach grumbled, and Michael rolled out of bed, grabbed a pair of sweats from his suitcase, and headed for the smaller bathroom. A shower, clean sweats, and he'd join Lily down in the kitchen unless she'd already made her way to her studio. He'd check in with her, then run a patrol on the house. Windows, doors, the fence line, and the rest of the small security measures would help keep Lily safe through the night. It also helped that he was a light sleeper and even more so when he was in a strange place.

Freshly washed and dressed, he made his way down to the kitchen a minute before Lily joined him.

"You were fast." She flashed a smile at him before she filled the kettle and set it on the stove to boil.

"Habit. You have to be able to get ready fast in my line of work, though admittedly I cheated." He gestured to the sweats before he glanced at her own. Normally he didn't like women in sweats, but he'd take her in anything she wore or didn't wear. His cock twitched at the image. Naked. Yeah, naked was always good, especially now he'd seen all her lithe lines and felt the small weight of her breasts in his hands.

"Did you want any tea?" Lily glanced over at him as she reached up to grab a mug.

"No thanks." Tea. Not something he'd ever been able to stomach. "Looks like there's coffee left; I'll heat it up." He gestured to the carafe.

"Don't know how you can drink that stuff." She shook her head and pulled out a second mug. "I'm going to throw some toast on. Not in the mood for anything heavy. I can grab eggs if you want something, or there are sandwich fixings in the fridge."

Yeah, food sounded like a great idea. "I can cook for myself if I want eggs. You're not supposed to wait on me."

Lily grinned. "And here I thought Dominant types liked being served."

"Some of us do. I prefer to keep my dominance in the bedroom." Unlike a couple of the people he knew, the idea of micromanaging a sub didn't appeal to him. "Oh sure, the occasional time, when the sub is naked or in lingerie and serving me dinner can be fun, but all day every day? Not my thing."

"Have you ever tried it?" Lily added two slices of bread to the toaster.

Michael turned away from her and headed to the fridge.

"Michael?"

"Yeah, once." His throat tightened. *Don't go there. Please don't go there.*

"What happened?"

"What do you have to do today?" *Change the subject. Yeah, that's going to work.*

Lily pulled out a chair from the small kitchen table and sat down. "Did something happen?"

Michael paused, one hand on the fridge door. "Yeah, you could say that." She wasn't going to let this drop. "It didn't go well." He forced himself to look back at her. "It's a long story, and you've got work to do."

"I'm waiting for my tea and toast, but if you don't want to talk about it right now, just say so."

Blunt. He liked that in a woman. "Fine, you're right. I don't want to talk about it. If we work out, if we want to see where this takes us, and I do, then we'll discuss it." No secrets. It was one of his rules when it came to relationships. You didn't keep secrets from your submissive. After all, how could you expect them to be honest with you if you weren't honest in return?

"If..." She sighed. "Yeah, we've both got to think about that one. You want to continue this, and I do too, but shouldn't we wait until the assignment is over?"

"If I had any sense, then yes, but when it comes to you, I don't think it exists, or I wouldn't have taken it this far with you." Was she ready to take that step with him? Hell, he didn't know if he was prepared to voice it, even though he'd accepted that he wanted Lily to be his. He turned, the fridge forgotten for the moment. "What we did felt right, and I have no regrets."

"That's good to hear, because I certainly don't regret it either." The chair scraped back across the floor as she rose and walked over to him. "Bad timing, yes; bad choice, no." She reached up and cupped his cheek even as the toaster clicked and popped two slices into the air. She turned, her attention caught by the sound, and the moment was done. "Tea, toast, work through the day, grab meals as needed, then bed. Separate beds."

Now that was a topic they'd discuss later, but he had no intention of sleeping apart from her tonight or any night to come.

Chapter Seven

Lily yawned and smiled at Michael's weight behind her. Once again, she'd woken in his bed, but this time she was partially dressed, and nothing more than sleep had taken place. Damn the man. He'd been stubborn once she'd finished her work for the night, and she'd been far too tired to argue with him. Oh, there'd been no sex involved. He'd promised as much and claimed he'd known how tired she was. So they'd slept together. Nothing more than that, and it felt right to wake up with Michael lying next to her. They were in his room, though, not hers. She wasn't ready for that step, to let him into the room she claimed as her own. A place she had never let a man into. It was her sanctuary. It had always been, and she doubted that would change anytime soon.

With a sigh, she snuggled into Michael, all too aware of the outline of his erect cock as it pressed against her buttocks. He was like most men, a hard-on just before he woke, and she wasn't about to complain. After all, she already knew he understood how to use it, and he wasn't pushing her to have sex right now. If his breathing was anything to go by, he was still asleep, but that would change, and she'd be ready for him.

Peaceful.

When had she last felt so at peace?

Before the appearance of the stalker; that was certain. Even with the stalker still in her life, she was safe with Michael. He'd never let anything harm her, not if he was in her life, but like all things, she knew what they now shared would come to an end. She could deal with that, as long as she kept a wall between them, Lily knew she would be able to cope when he walked out of her life when the assignment was over and done with.

Her heart sank at the idea, and she took a deep breath. No, she wasn't about to worry about the time they had left together. Better to enjoy what they had and deal with the fallout when it happened.

Shadows of the Past

Until then, she wouldn't let herself think about it.

Lily closed her eyes and relaxed. She'd be up soon enough, as would he. Perhaps they would indulge themselves before she had to begin her work for the day, but she wasn't about to wake him up and—

A soft click from downstairs, the noise familiar, caught her attention, and she stiffened. *The door. That's the front door.*

Michael shifted behind her, one hand pressed against Lily's shoulder. "I'll check it out." A moment later he rolled out of bed, his feet silent on the bedroom floor as he moved to the door.

Naked.

Was he planning on going downstairs without pulling something on, and what the hell was that in his hand?

Her gaze narrowed as she glanced at him.

A handgun?

She hadn't heard him open a drawer any more than she had heard his steps.

Lily moved on the bed, and he looked back at her, one finger pressed to his lips. He frowned, then pointed at her and then at the bed. Her jaw clenched, but she nodded her agreement. The last thing she wanted to do was get in the way when Michael was doing his job.

Silently Michael slipped out of the room, and she lost sight of him a few seconds later, though the bedroom door was half open. She listened, but there was nothing, not even a creak on the stairs, which meant he'd figured out how to move up and down them without hitting the one squeaky floorboard. Lily eased her way to the edge of the bed.

What's going on? She strained, unable to hear anything. Maybe there'd been nothing there, and they'd both been woken by nothing more than a creak in the house? No, she knew the sound. It had been the front door. The click was a noise she knew all too well.

A loud crash echoed through the house, and she sprang to her feet, sweats forgotten as she ran to the door. Lily was halfway down the stairs before her brain put the pieces together.

Broken glass.

No gunshot, and there hadn't been a silencer on Michael's gun; he hadn't fired at anyone. Could there have been a shot from the outside, from a distance? No, she'd have heard it, wouldn't she?

"Stop," Michael snapped.

Lily froze on the second to last step.

"I told you to stay upstairs." His tone cold and distant.

"I know, but I heard a crack. It sounded like broken glass, and I...I didn't think." She flushed and peered around. Where was he? The door into the front room was open, a place she rarely used except for the occasional visitor. She kept to the back of the house most of the time, where she had access to her backyard from her studio.

"Go back upstairs and call the cops. Get hold of that detective if you have his direct number. Tell them you've had something thrown through the window, and we think it's the stalker."

"Are you all right?" Fear chilled her flesh. Why wasn't he coming back into her line of sight?

"Yes, but there's a lot of glass, and I don't want you down here." His voice sounded strained, and she was tempted to disobey him.

"Now, Lily."

Without further hesitation, she turned and fled back up the stairs. The stalker. Michael had to have a decent reason to think the person behind the broken glass was the stalker, but she had nothing to go on except his word. Did she trust his skills? She'd trusted him in bed, and he'd found the footprint, so she had no reason not to. But if the stalker had escalated to throwing things through the window, then hopefully the police would finally take the situation seriously.

God, she could only hope so. If this didn't do the trick, she hated to think what would have to happen for them to investigate this thoroughly.

Lily sat down on the edge of her bed, picked up the phone, and made the call.

Shadows of the Past

* * * *

A mistake. Entering the house and then breaking the window had been a mistake, but he'd had to see for himself. The cameras hadn't been enough. While he'd watched the events on the screen, he'd been able to deny what was happening, but in person?

How could she do this to him? Sleep with that bastard? The security guy was supposed to protect her, not fall into bed with her. Wasn't it against some sort of code to seduce a client? Could he be struck off, barred, stripped of his credentials, or something similar?

His heart pounded, breath ragged as he continued to pedal his bike. At least he'd used his common sense and avoided using a car. Cars had engines. Engines could be heard by other people, but another guy out for a fast ride was just that, a cyclist getting his ride in before work. Oh, he'd been careful there, picked out basic black cycling shorts and a plain black shirt with a matching helmet. Common enough around here with a number of health nuts in the area. Even his bike was generic, so if Michael had caught a glimpse of it, the man would be unlikely to have seen enough details to describe it.

Yes, he'd been both careful and stupid.

His Lily, his sweet, perfect Lily. She'd truly been with Michael, and he had to keep to the plan. Use Michael to get to Lily, but now there was a personal aspect. Michael had touched her. More than that, from the sounds coming from the hallway. He'd spanked her when they'd gone into his room. How could she have allowed such a perversion?

His stomach knotted as he focused on cycling, picking up speed until he reached a corner and stopped peddling long enough to make the turn.

His car. It would be another five minutes or more before he reached the car. He had sufficient time to calm down and think things through.

He glanced back over his shoulder.

Nothing. He wasn't being followed, and the route he'd taken

avoided most of the cameras. By now it wouldn't matter if he was picked up. They wouldn't think to look this far out for whoever had broken the window. If they checked at all.

Michael. He'd laid hands on Lily. Perhaps there'd been force involved, an incident he hadn't picked up in his surveillance?

Yes, of course, it was the only thing that made sense. His Lily wouldn't have committed such a mistake if she hadn't been pressured into it. She was too soft-hearted, and now it had come back to bite her. So why hadn't she called Michael's boss? Did the man have something on her?

Anger built with each passing moment, and he forced his breathing to calm as he slowed his pace. Almost to the car. He'd be out of the area soon enough, and then he could work on setting Michael up. But for what? It had to be something that would encourage him to leave Lily alone.

No, more than that. He needed to break the man, destroy him for what he'd done to Lily. He'd rescue his Lily, and then she would turn to him once and for all. How could she do anything but that when he would have rescued her from an abusive asshole? He'd have to lay a careful trail of breadcrumbs; there was no point in being sloppy at this point. He'd already made too many mistakes by stepping into the house when Michael was present. He wouldn't repeat it. No, it was time to start using his brain instead of being run by his desires.

* * * *

Michael swore under his breath as he looked around the front room, a room he had only been in once before to check for security reasons since he'd begun his work with Lily. Glass covered the floor—large shards, small shards, whole pieces glinted in the light from the streets. This wasn't going to be easy to clean up. He sighed and checked his legs. Small cuts marred his bare thighs, but he couldn't feel them. No doubt he would later.

Was he hurt anywhere else? He glanced at his arms and torso. Minor cuts again, nothing anywhere near his cock, which was a

91

blessing, but he couldn't stand in the middle of broken glass until the cops arrived. Especially not like this. A soft noise upstairs made it clear Lily was making the call, which meant he needed to move.

He turned slowly, taking care not to place his feet directly on any visible glass, but that was the problem with glass. You couldn't always see the shards until it was too late. He smacked on the light as he entered the hall and tried not to jar the pieces in his flesh. The small ones would dig their way into his body, and he wouldn't find them until it was too late unless he was careful to remove them early on. He winced at the thought, his Glock still in his right hand as he made his way out of the room. Damnit all. He'd have a dozen or more splinters he'd need to pull out of his skin.

"Lily, can you toss me down my sweats? And I'm going to need tweezers."

"Sure." A moment later, she appeared at the top of the stairs and tossed the sweats down. "It'll take me a minute to get the tweezers."

"Okay, when you bring them down, don't leave the stairs. There's glass everywhere, and the police are going to want to see the scene before we clean up." Photos. They'd want pictures of the glass and his injuries, as minor as they were.

"Understood." She glanced down at him, and for a moment he caught sight of his Lily. His cock surged, balls tight against the base of his erection. He swallowed and forced himself to turn away. Dressed in only a T-shirt and positioned at the top of the stairs, she had given him a clear view all the way to heaven. "Put something on, Lily. I don't need to be distracted right now, and I certainly don't want the cops to see you like this."

"On… Oh." He could hear the blush behind her words even as she scurried out of sight.

Michael bit back a chuckle and sat down on the second to bottom stair. "I need a phone. I have to take pictures of the glass in my legs before I dress. Cops will want records." But he had no desire to sit and wait in the buff until they showed up. He set his Glock to the right and winced as he got a better look at the injuries. Dozens of small and not so small pieces of glass glittered in his legs and arms. His right leg and arm had taken the worst of it, and sitting down on the step had also told him he had at least one or two pieces in his right buttock, which meant there would be pieces in or around his hip.

Light steps behind him alerted Michael to Lily's presence, and he glanced over his shoulder. She'd thrown her sweats on and stuffed her feet into a pair of deck shoes. "I have them." She stopped a step above him and passed the phone and tweezers down.

It didn't take long to snap the pictures he needed, but by the time it was done, he could hear the sirens approaching the house. With a scowl, he pulled on his sweats. "Take this upstairs. I don't want them thinking they need to take my gun for any reason." He unloaded the clip and checked the chamber before he handed the Glock off. The cops didn't know him, and he didn't want his first meeting with the locals to include him being cuffed and his gun taken until it was cleared.

Barefooted and still covered in glass beneath the sweats, he stood and waited for their arrival even as Lily fled back upstairs only to return as the cars drew up. He glanced at Lily and nodded once. "It's going to be all right."

She didn't say anything but inclined her head as she waited on the stairs.

Michael walked gingerly to the front door and opened it before he stepped aside and waved the police in. Two uniforms and a middle-aged man in a rumpled suit entered. It didn't take long to explain the situation, and Michael kept his answers short, calm, and honest, except for the part where he'd brought a gun downstairs with him. Nor did he mention he'd been in the same bed as Lily, not something he wanted in a police report, for Lily's sake if nothing else.

"So, you're the hired protection?" Detective Keith Richmond met Michael's gaze.

Shadows of the Past

"Yeah, been here two nights now." Michael kept a calm smile in place as he replied.

"You were upstairs when you heard the front door."

Michael had been through this with the uniformed officers, but he knew the drill. The detective wanted to catch him in a lie. "Yes, in my bed. There was a click that sounded like the front door. A door I knew to be locked as I'd double checked all doors and windows before retiring for the night."

Richmond tipped his head to the left and nodded once. "I see. What did you do then?"

"I went downstairs to find out what had happened. The door slammed, but I thought I saw something in the front room, stepped inside, and that's when a rock crashed through the window."

"What did you see that made you step into the other room instead of following the intruder?"

Michael frowned and closed his eyes as he tried to piece it together. There'd been something. Not a movement but a flash? No, not a flash, a glimmer. The movement that hadn't fit with the room or the situation. "I'm not sure. Could have been a reflection." Except he wasn't sure what could have been there to cause one.

"All right. So, you stayed put after the window was broken. Any injuries?"

"Minor. Glass in my arms and legs, but I'll be able to tend to those myself. I have pictures for you if you need them for your report."

"We prefer to collect our own, and for that, we'll need you to come with us to the hospital, or we can call for an ambulance if needed."

Michael arched an eyebrow but kept his tone even. "Am I being arrested?"

"No, Mr. Parker." Richmond's lips twitched into a half smile.

"Then you can collect your pictures here. I'll tend my injuries and remain with my charge." He nodded up the stairs toward Lily.

"Ah yes, Ms. Elliot. I'll need to speak with you directly, though

I understand the uniforms have already taken a basic statement."

"They have," Lily agreed as she rested one hand on the banister. "I don't know how much I could add to that, but you know I'm willing to cooperate. The sooner this person is found the faster I can return to a more normal life."

"Perhaps you could persuade Mr. Parker to accompany us to the hospital. I can always leave an officer in his place and—"

"You'd try to leave an officer, but all it takes is a call, and he'd be pulled away. Thank you, Detective Richmond, but I agree with Mr. Parker," Lily cut in but didn't raise her voice. She sighed and rubbed the back of her neck. "Look, I know you have things you want to get done, and we'll cooperate, but not if it means leaving me alone. You couldn't even get your captain to see there was a problem, and I doubt he's going to change his mind. Richmond will chalk the broken window up to kids and claim we both overreacted to natural sounds in the house. I know the drill by now."

The older man turned to watch the two uniformed officers continue their walkthrough of the front room, but Michael was all too aware Richmond was buying himself time. Richmond appeared, at first glance, to be in his forties, stocky but not overweight, with thinning brown hair and gray-green eyes. His pants weren't suit pants as Michael had thought initially but separate dress pants with a crinkled appearance, along with a shirt and jacket. Professional but overworked, that was how the detective came across. However, it didn't stop the man from being good at his job.

"All right, we've got the pictures we need from the scene, and I'll have uniforms check the outside and the surrounding area, but we all know the person behind this is no longer in the area." Richmond turned to look back at them. "Did you hear a car, or do you think they left on foot?"

Had there been anything? No engine sounds. Michael had been certain of that, but what about footsteps? He frowned and went over the background noise. There'd been something out there, a sound he should have known.

Shadows of the Past

"No car, but they left too quickly to be entirely on foot. Maybe a bike?" Even as he said it the pieces fell into place. The sound of a chain. "Yes, a bicycle. I can't add anything more." The flash of movement when the intruder had left, the movement... Michael's instincts said a man, and the shape of his head suggested a bike helmet, but the rest was little more than a blur. In time, the pieces might fall into place, but he couldn't push it. The memory would clear or it wouldn't. There was no middle ground.

"A bike? Interesting. I'll have the officers check and see if there's any sign, and we'll pull up the nearest traffic cams, see what we can find." Richmond inclined his head. He slipped a card from his pocket and handed it to Michael. "If you can email the pictures to me it would help. That said, I'd like to take some of my own. If you're not willing to go to the hospital with me and have official pictures taken, I can't guarantee the images would be allowed into court when we catch this guy."

Lily took a step down and rested a hand on his shoulder. "A bike? There's a lot of them in the area, bike clubs and the like. Damnit, I should have put cameras up when this mess began."

"You can't see into the future, Lily." Without thinking Michael reached back and rested one hand on hers.

Richmond's eyes widened, then narrowed. "Well, we'll see what we can find. You don't want to be in the front room without decent thick-soled shoes on. I can't express how easy it is to cut yourself on hidden shards. You'll be cleaning up in there for weeks. Just when you think it's all gone, you'll find a small shard in the sole of your foot. So, be careful in there, and don't go in without shoes for at least a month."

"What if I hired a professional cleaning company?"

"They can't guarantee they'll be able to get it all either, even if they claim otherwise," Richmond explained. "Glass gets everywhere. You'll need to get something over the gap and call someone to replace the window first thing in the morning."

Morning.

Michael glanced at the time on his phone. They weren't far off that now. Five a.m. Another four hours, and businesses would be open. At least it was Monday morning instead of the weekend, which meant they had a better chance of getting workmen out to handle the repairs.

"I'll need to call Daniel. He'll have to be brought up to speed on what's happened." Lily sat down on the stairs behind him but didn't lean in. "God, this is a mess. I don't understand why the stalker would go from gifts to this right now."

Richmond met Michael's gaze. "I think Mr. Parker knows, but I'll leave that discussion between the pair of you."

Michael's heart sank. He hadn't wanted to think about it, about the reason for the escalation. Yet there was only one thing he could identify as a trigger. The stalker knew Michael had taken Lily to his bed, and whoever the man was, he wasn't happy about the situation.

Shadows of the Past

Chapter Eight

"This is insane." Lily sighed as she considered the state of the front room. Glass glittered everywhere, from small shards to larger pieces that would be easier to pick up, but Richmond had been right. She'd be avoiding glass for weeks if not months to come.

"You don't have to handle it alone, Lily." Michael moved behind her and rested a hand on her shoulder.

She leaned into his touch and sighed. At least Michael understood her, or so it seemed. He didn't talk down to her, didn't try to slip his hands into her sweats. Instead, he offered support and nothing more. It would have been all too easy to turn and throw herself into his arms, but she was still too shaken. Any decisions she made now couldn't include sex or relationships, not when she understood she wasn't thinking entirely straight and was likely suffering from a mild form of shock.

"We've got company," Michael warned as he moved his hand and stepped back from her a moment before the front door opened.

"Lily, oh God. Are you all right? What happened?" Daniel Walker stormed in, but he wasn't alone. A step behind him was the assistant who'd been at the sip-and-paint, John Wash. "John, get the coffee going. We need to get this place cleaned up."

Which meant Daniel would avoid most of the work, and John would spend the time running around, trying to pick up the slack Daniel left behind.

"I'm fine. Michael was here and heard the intruder. I hate to think what would happen if Michael hadn't been here."

"Yes, yes, of course, Michael." Daniel pulled Lily into a hug. "I'm sure he was helpful."

She stiffened. "Don't, please. I don't think I can take being touched right now." She pressed her hands to Daniel's chest and tried to break contact.

"Don't be silly. This is for the best. You need to know you're safe right now." Daniel refused to let her go.

"She said she doesn't want to be touched." Michael stepped closer.

"I know Lily better than you ever will," Daniel snapped but released his grip on Lily. "But fine, fine. I don't want an argument."

Lily's heart raced, and a slight tremble ran through her body. Why hadn't Daniel let go of her when she'd told him to? *Because he thinks he knows what's best for me.* It was far more than her being his client; he had a need to treat her like a child. It had to end. There was no way she could tell him right now, not in a way that would force Daniel to listen to her. She nibbled on her bottom lip and looked away from him.

"We need to get this cleaned up, and the glazier—" Lily began.

"Is already on the way," John cut into the conversation as he walked back in from the kitchen. "Sorry, Lily, I didn't mean to interrupt. I assumed it would be for the best to get that part sorted as quickly as possible. You don't want an open hole in the front of your house."

She flashed a smile at the other man. At least he understood the difference between taking over and helping. "No, you did the right thing. Now we need to get the worst of this glass cleaned up."

Thirty minutes into the work, the glazier arrived, and John stepped in to deal with the man after he checked with Lily first. Daniel sat at the kitchen table with his laptop and barely even looked up as the men continued to work, but Lily didn't speak to him. Having that discussion now would only add to her stress—not something she wanted to do anytime soon. God, she had to. Whatever had been between them in the form of a professional relationship had to come to an end. If nothing else, this entire business with the stalker had convinced her of that. Instead of working with them, helping with the cleanup, Daniel was on his laptop. It was the same during any events he deigned to show up to; he was either on his phone, laptop, or a tablet.

She tried to pinpoint when things had changed, but in truth, the shift from an active manager and friend to background noise and more trouble than he was worth had happened over time. Now it was too obvious to ignore.

"Don't mind Daniel. He's been busy juggling a lot of clients of late, and I think he's having a few personal problems." John moved close to Lily as they worked to remove the glass shards.

The glaziers were busy nailing a series of boards over the broken window. They were ordering the replacement glass, but it would take a day or two before they'd have it in hand, and the two men the company had sent out were quickly making the house as secure as possible. At least it was one thing she didn't have to worry about, and as far as she could see it would be a lot harder for the stalker to gain access through the window with the thick boards in place. Still, she didn't like the idea of having wood in place of glass, even for a short time.

"Lily?" John pressed.

"Sorry, yes. Daniel's taken on more clients?"

"About forty now. Most of them performing artists." John used the hand vacuum to collect smaller shards, and the low noise cut through their ability to chat for a time.

Forty other clients? Well, it explained why he was always busy, and she had come to accept she wouldn't be his only concern, but that many new contracts? It at least explained why he needed both an assistant and several office staff. John fell somewhere between the lines of senior office manager and agent, often taking care of the things Daniel used to do for her. Now the pieces fell into place, and she glanced back toward the hall.

Was Daniel still busy on his laptop?

"Why did he bother showing up if he's going to stay out in the kitchen?" she asked when John shut the hand vacuum off.

"To make a show of being in charge. It's how Daniel's been of late." John emptied the vacuum into a large, thick garbage bag. "A good manager always appears to be interested in his clients, even if his focus is elsewhere. It's something he's fond of saying, at least in the office." John glanced around the room. "This is going to take a while."

Three hours later, they'd cleaned up the worst of it, and her body refused to let her do any more. With a groan, she rolled out her shoulders and looked around. Michael had handled the hauling and any of the heavy-duty work. John had helped with the detail work, but Daniel had remained in the kitchen except to tell John they needed more coffee and tell Lily off for risking her hands with handling the glass. He hadn't even noticed she'd worn gloves the entire time.

"You need a break." Michael slid his cell phone back into his pocket and picked up the last of the bags. "And you might want to talk to your manager about contacting your clients. This is going to push you back workwise."

Lily groaned and closed her eyes. She hadn't given a thought to the outstanding commissions. She couldn't work today. Even if she did, she was in the wrong headspace now, and anything she tried to do wouldn't be her best. Paying clients deserved her best at all times, and she wasn't about to damage her reputation by turning in substandard work.

"Damnit, you're right. Only hope Daniel sees it the same way." If he didn't, then what?

It's my work. I'm the one in charge, not Daniel. Maybe it was time he realized that, but from how Daniel had been acting, he'd forgotten.

"You won't be on your own." Michael didn't move any closer to her but instead shifted the bag in his grip. "Give me five minutes, and I'll be right with you."

"No, I can do it alone." She had to, or Daniel would always see her as a child to be managed each step of the way. "Thank you though. I appreciate it."

Michael caught and held her gaze, his eyes narrowing, before he gave a single nod and walked out with the bag. That he'd wanted to stay with her was evident, but the fact he'd given her a chance to handle this on her own spoke volumes. He cared for her but didn't want to squash her spirit.

Rare and beautiful.

Though she doubted he would ever agree to being called beautiful. It wasn't a word most men believed applied to them.

With a slight smile struggling to claim her lips, she straightened her back and walked into the kitchen.

"Yes, I know, but you agreed to the contract, Nina. If you let them down, they won't try to hire you again, and it could be months before anything else comes up. Word gets around quickly in this industry." Daniel held a cell phone to his ear and nodded at Lily when she entered the room.

She glanced around the kitchen and scowled. Drawers were open, cupboard doors left ajar, and one of the counters was now covered in stains, spilled grounds, and sugar. A quick look at the table told her it wasn't much better. What did the man think he was doing? This was her home, her world, not his, but he'd sprawled his things out in the room without care.

And maybe he didn't.

Fine, it was another reason she needed to sever ties with him or at least get him to hand over her files to John.

As Daniel continued his conversation in a tone Lily was all too familiar with, Lily tried to clean up some of the mess that threatened to devastate her kitchen. She hadn't gone any further than closing two cupboards when she heard the conversation come to an end.

"Everything all right, Lily? The room finished with?"

"The cleaning is as done as it's going to be, or at least I assumed so before I saw this." She turned and met Daniel's gaze.

"What do you mean?" He set the phone down and looked around. "Nothing a couple of minutes' work won't see to."

"Fine, then get up and do it." She folded her arms beneath her breasts.

"What? No, you can't be serious." Daniel closed his laptop. "I'm not—"

"Yes, you are. You made the mess; you can clean it up." If he believed he was going to walk away and leave her with the kitchen to clean up, he had another thing coming. "You've sat in here, turned my kitchen upside down while I worked with Michael and John to clean the front room. The only reason you showed up was to appear involved, but a word of advice, if you want to look good to a client, you get off your ass and pitch in. You don't take over my kitchen and get on with working with your other clients and turn the place upside down in the process and then have the nerve to expect me to clean up after you."

Daniel opened his mouth to protest, but she cut him off.

"With that in mind, you're going to contact everyone who you've signed contracts with on my behalf, something you never had written permission to do, and you'll let them know all work is being pushed back by a week. If there are penalties, you're paying them out of your money, not mine."

"Oh no, we have to discuss this, kid. You're overreacting, and I can understand it after all you've been through. But you can't honestly expect me to do that. It's bad for business." He smiled and rose from the chair. "Let's talk about this."

"I've told you not to call me kid." What the hell was wrong with the man? "Once you've talked to the clients, you're going to turn my files over to John, and we're going to change the contract. I'll be talking to a lawyer before I sign anything, and you will cease taking on work in my name." A weight lifted from her chest as she finally unleashed on Daniel.

"Lily, please, you need time to think about all of this. I'll call the clients and discuss a couple of days' delay."

"You're not listening to me, Daniel. I said a week, and I'm not backing down on this. I've been working every day for the last two years. Don't you understand how exhausted I am? How close I am to burning out?" No, of course, he didn't see it. "I need time to recover, and this shit with the stalker only adds to my stress. A stalker

Shadows of the Past

you didn't even believe existed. If you can't respect my choice, then I'll be forced to leave your agency immediately."

MICHAEL HAULED THE bag out to the garbage and looked around. How had the stalker gotten into the house? *A key, you moron.* He swore under his breath and turned to peer at the front door. How many people had keys? Her manager or agent, whatever he called himself, had one, but who else? Could someone in Daniel's office have copied the key? If so, the stalker had full access to the house.

Shit, Michael didn't like where this was going.

By now Daniel should have contacted Harvey with the details about the rest of the staff working for the agency, and Michael knew he needed to talk to his boss anyway. He'd called Harvey initially after the police had left, but the older man hadn't been in the office.

He slipped out the phone and made the call, all the time hoping he was wrong about the situation.

"Yes?"

"Harvey, any leads on the shoe print?"

Harvey coughed and cleared his throat. "Emailing you the details. How's the cleanup going? I caught your message earlier."

At least that was one thing: he wouldn't have to go over all the details of the early-morning events. "Slowly, but we're getting there. I had a thought, one I don't like, but the intruder must have used a key. Right now, according to information Lily shared with me, the only other person who has a key is Daniel. Is it possible someone from his agency made a copy?"

"Yeah, and that opens up a can of worms. He sent over the list of employees, and there are a couple on there with criminal records. Looks like Mr. Walker isn't too fussy about who he hires." Harvey growled his displeasure at the situation. "One at least has had a restraining order placed against him from a former girlfriend."

And all of that had been ignored? "Shit, anything else come up on the search?"

"One petty theft, another with a drinking habit, and then there's Daniel himself. It appears he's been playing fast and loose with his clients funds, or so Mags thinks. She's checking further into the situation, but it's not looking good."

"Shit." Michael turned and glanced at the door. "Someone's coming. I'll touch base with you later." He ended the call and put his phone away as Daniel stalked out of the house, his backpack over his shoulder, though it was still half open and the corner of his laptop stuck out of one side.

"It's your fault. Lily listened to me before you walked into her life. What the hell do you think you're doing in there?" Daniel closed the distance between them and stepped into Michael's personal space. "What are you doing to her? Have you fucked her, is that it? Yes, of course, you've pulled her into your bed, and now look at us. You've ruined my working relationship with her. Well, I'm going to report you to your boss. I'll have you fired. Got it? Fired!" He shoved two fingers against Michael's chest.

Michael reacted without hesitation. He grabbed Daniel by the wrist and twisted Daniel's hand away from his chest. "Don't."

"Don't get you fired? After the way you just manhandled me?" Daniel tried to pull his hand free, but Michael refused to release his grasp. "This is assault."

"No, this is restraining you. Assault is a whole different ball game, and believe me, you don't want to find out how that feels." Michael forced his voice to remain cold and calm. "She's made her choice, and I suggest you come to terms with it. I don't know what she said to you, but I wasn't in the room and had nothing to do with it." However, if she'd fired Daniel, so much the better. Had Daniel stolen funds from Lily? Michael would discuss it with her and do his best to convince her to hire a forensic accountant.

"Let go of me," Daniel snapped.

Michael smiled and released his grip on the man. "Touch me again, and I'll defend myself. Is that clear?"

Daniel's top lip curled in a snarl. "Perfectly. You're banging her.

Shadows of the Past

You might even be behind this entire stalking thing. All a ploy to—"

"To do what? Be hired as her protection? How the hell would I make sure she hired Harvey Brent's firm? You're not making sense, Mr. Walker. There are other companies she might have reached out to, and I didn't even know who Ms. Elliot was until Harvey handed me the file." The man was insane. Michael paused and took a step back from Daniel. No, not crazy. Angry and upset. If he was skimming money from his clients, then he was intelligent enough not to alert them. Insanity and intelligence could go hand in hand, but in this case, Michael doubted it.

Shit, this wasn't his specialty. Mags knew how to dig into situations like this. Then it would be a case of turning it over to the cops if Lily didn't hire her own accountant.

"I suggest you leave and calm down." Michael nodded toward the gate. "If Lily wants to talk to you, she'll call you. If not, I suggest you leave her be."

Daniel slammed the gate behind him. The man didn't say a word directly to Michael, who watched as the agent got into his car and left. Had John come in the same car, or did he have his own? Typical of Daniel to think only of himself, but that had been the impression Michael had had of the man from the first.

"He's gone," Michael announced as he walked into the kitchen and paused in the doorway. Lily was sitting at the table, head in her hands, her body racked with shakes. Soft sounds filled the room, and it took a moment before he realized she was crying. Without a word, he moved and pulled her up into his arms, one hand pressed against the back of her head. "Hey now, it's all right. Whatever happened, it's all right." He didn't know what else he said at that moment. The words spilled out as he moved a hand up and down her back. "I'm right here. You're not alone. You don't have to deal with this on your own anymore."

Was she listening to him? He had no way of knowing as she sobbed in his arms, her breathing ragged.

"Didn't— didn't want to do it," Lily finally stammered.

"Daniel, right? He didn't take it very well." Had Daniel shouted at Lily? God, if the man had verbally assaulted her, Michael would track him down and teach the bastard a lesson. Odd, he hadn't heard raised voices, but it didn't mean Daniel hadn't said something cruel.

"I did it. I told Daniel I didn't want to work directly with him anymore." Her tears slowly eased, and she gulped for air. "Daniel was so angry with me once he realized I was serious. He thinks I'm a child. A little girl he needs to control."

Control, yes, but not in the same way Michael wanted to. His way wouldn't have left Lily upset like this. His way was consensual. Daniel's wasn't. "You're not a little girl. You're my Lily, and I don't like to see you hurt." He smoothed his hands over her hair, her back and down to her buttocks before he held her. She didn't need anything sexual at this moment, even if he wanted to take her to bed and show her it was all right now. He would protect her, keep her safe, and never let anyone hurt her if he had any say in the matter.

"I'll be okay. I know I'll be fine. Daniel's angry with me right now, but he knows he's in the wrong." She lifted her head, her eyes red-rimmed. "I hope he knows he was wrong." Her bottom lip caught between her teeth. "Maybe he doesn't. God, could he believe he was right, working me to the bone and taking on all those contracts without checking with me first?"

There was more she needed to know, but was this the right time? She was already in a bad place. Shit, Michael couldn't keep anything from her. It wouldn't be right. It went against the idea of honesty between a Dominant and his sub.

"Is everything okay?" A male voice broke through Michael's thoughts.

Lily tensed in his arms. "John?"

"Yes, I heard something and..." John paused. "Have you been crying?"

Daniel released his hold on Lily, though it was the last thing he wanted to do, and turned to look at John. "She had a fight with

Shadows of the Past

Daniel, and she's a bit shaken."

"A fight. Oh God, what about? Did you fire him?" John's eyes narrowed, his jaw tight as his gaze moved between Michael and Lily.

"Sort of. I've fired him but not the agency." Lily scuffed a hand beneath her eyes and pushed back her hair. "I've asked him to transfer my file over to you after he's taken care of a few things for me first."

"And Michael?" Twin spots of heat flared across John's cheeks.

"Michael was being a friend, exactly like you would have been if you'd walked in and seen me like that."

Her words were straightforward and honest, so why did Michael's heart sink and his gut knot when she spoke?

A friend. I want to be more than a friend. Does she want the same thing, or is this her way of telling me there can never be anything more between us?

Chapter Nine

Lily ached from head to foot as she stepped out into the backyard. Cleanup had taken the rest of the day, and even then, she was aware there would be pieces of glass she would have to watch for. The work had gone quicker than it would have done thanks to Michael and John, but they'd worked mostly in silence after John had walked in on them in the kitchen.

Talk about awkward.

At least John hadn't said anything nasty. With everything else that had happened during the day, it wouldn't have surprised her if John had lashed out at her after the scene with Daniel.

Daniel. Shit, she hadn't followed up with him to make sure he'd contacted her clients.

Lily pulled out her phone and checked the time. It was too late to call him now, not without making it appear as if she was trying to patch things up between them. Better to keep things to business hours and avoid any misunderstandings. Odds were, Daniel was still angry with her, and she didn't want to end up in tears again.

Her back and shoulders throbbed, but it was understandable with the combination of disturbed night, the fight with Daniel, and the work clearing the glass. Now all she wanted to do was sink into a warm bath and try to soak away her stress. Maybe with a glass of wine?

Yes, a large glass. Hot water. Bubbles. Lots of bubbles.

Strong arms wrapped around her as she was pulled back against Michael's chest, and she tensed. Even though she knew it was him from the feel of his arms and his scent, she couldn't force herself to relax.

"Is there something wrong?" Michael nuzzled her neck, his lips soft and warm against her skin.

Lily pulled free from his hold and turned to look at him. How could she explain what was going on when she barely understood it? "I need time to think after today's events. It's just, I don't know what we're doing here." She rubbed the back of her neck and tried to put her thoughts into order.

"I'm protecting you. It's what I've been hired to do." Michael didn't move toward her, though confusion flickered across his features.

"That's not what I'm talking about, Michael. I mean what we did yesterday." She nodded toward the house. "Is it a one-time thing or something more? I'm not sure if I even want to know at this point."

"A one-off, is that what you think I wanted from you?"

Wanted, past tense. Lily's heart sank. "I don't know what to believe right now."

"It's been a long day for both of us, but regardless of what's happened, I need you to understand. I have no interest in a one-time thing. I couldn't ever think that with you. Lily, I know none of this makes sense, especially for me, but I've wanted you from the minute I saw your pictures in the file. I tried to believe it was nothing more than an impulse, but meeting you in person made it clear. There's something I can't explain, but this feels right with you."

Why wouldn't it make sense for him? "I'm not entirely following you here. No, it doesn't matter. I'm not ready for this. I need some space, a little time to work through all of this. The stalker, Daniel, the broken window, us—whatever this is between us. I need to clear my head before I make a mistake."

"Is that what you think it was, what we did, a mistake?"

Had she said it had been a mistake? Lily frowned and stared at her home. The one place where she should have been safe and yet couldn't be, not with the stalker still out there.

"It's not what I meant." She sighed, and her shoulders dropped as she struggled to make sense of her thoughts. No, this wasn't the time or the place. "I'm going to go inside, run a bath, relax with a glass of wine, and then go to bed. Alone." She lifted her gaze and met his. "Please, give me time to deal with all of this."

Michael fell silent; his gaze narrowed, tension building across his shoulders. For a moment, he didn't move; then the tension eased, and he nodded once. "All right. I'm not going to pressure you, Lily. I'm here if you need me, but I want you to think about one thing. I have no desire to push you, but I don't intend to turn my back on you and walk away. I want you. I need you in my life, but the choice must be yours. Take tonight. Take as many nights as you need. I'll still be here when you want to talk." He closed the gap between them. "May I touch you?"

She closed her eyes. A touch was dangerous. She might make a mistake and let it become something more right now, but she wanted to feel Michael's hands on her. "Yes." She didn't open her eyes as he brushed one hand against her left cheek and slid his grip up into her hair. His body. She could feel it close. A welcome heat radiated from him as he wrapped his other arm around Lily and pulled her against his chest.

Her muscles tightened, then relaxed. Michael's touch felt right even as her mind screamed a warning. She wouldn't give in to whatever existed between them, not this time. She had to have space between them, if only for one night. Her body might crave him, but her heart and mind needed a chance to heal. Needed a moment to recover from the events of the last twenty-four hours.

Lips brushed across hers, and they parted beneath his touch. Her eyes never opened as she leaned in to the tender invasion of Michael's tongue and lips. Heat rippled through her body as the lingering remains of any tension eased from her body. Her nipples hardened; heat built within her core as she surrendered to the kiss.

In his arms, she could forget everything she had been through, but it wasn't what she needed right now. Lily knew she had to end the kiss. With a sigh, she pressed her hands against his chest and pushed, the movement tender but enough to break the contact between their lips.

"Thank you," she murmured even as she opened her eyes.

He cupped her chin, his gaze gentle. "I'll give you all the time you need."

Shadows of the Past

She welcomed his touch. Even though she was safe in his arms, she couldn't think clearly. Her life, her choices—they all had to come without his interference. "Tomorrow. We should be able to talk tomorrow when I've been able to sort through all of this." She sighed as she pulled away from his hand before she walked back into her house.

A hot bath, a glass of wine, and a good night's sleep would put her in a better headspace.

* * * *

He growled and lashed out, his hand connecting with a lamp. The force of the blow sent it across the room to shatter against the wall. Shards scattered over the floor, but he didn't care. Anger ruled his actions as he turned and searched for something else to destroy. Mugs flew, books scattered, a chair tossed onto its side, and still his rage burned through him.

It wasn't supposed to be like this.

After all their years together, Lily should have turned to him, not turned on him. Betrayed and abandoned. It was the only thing that made sense.

Michael. The bastard had damaged what was between Lily and himself. Oh, he'd seen it now, not only the screen. No, this time he'd seen it in person, the look they'd shared and the way Michael had reacted.

The bastard had corrupted his precious Lily.

He couldn't let this go on. He had to find a way of bringing her back into his arms, his safety. If it meant he had to kill Michael, then so be it.

Could he do it? Could he kill a man?

Maybe he wouldn't have to kill Michael, only make him go away.

A call to the man's boss might work, but that was only a temporary measure. No, he had to do something that would prevent Michael from ever getting near her again.

Hurt him, destroy him, but not kill him. Not unless there was no other way.

His mind began to race, ideas hitting him faster than he could keep track of them.

He had to remove Michael from Lily's life once and for all, and then she'd turn to him because there would be no one else she could lean on. He'd cut off any other lines of support first, including that damned cop.

A few calls to the captain?

Calls could be traced, and maybe he didn't need to deal with the cop directly. There were other crimes in the area. All he had to do was drop a few hints that Michael was behind the stalking to begin with or that he was a would-be boyfriend. Either option might be enough to discredit anything Michael said.

He frowned and shook his head. No, there were pieces he'd need to work out. Cops weren't dumb. They wouldn't buy Michael as the stalker. The security agent hadn't been in the area when it had begun.

All he had to do was line them up in the right way for it to work. He'd prove himself to Lily, make it clear he was the only one who'd ever been there for her, and there was nothing Michael or anyone else could do to stop them from being together.

Lily was his.

* * * *

Michael turned and watched as Lily walked back into the house. God, how he wanted to follow her in and find a way to persuade her to stay with him, where he could protect her. He needed her, truly needed her, even if he hadn't had the balls to tell her outright. She was all he'd ever wanted in life and more besides, but was this the right time or place to fall in love?

Love?

There was never a right time, and he'd learned it the hard way when he'd been younger. Shit, that had been with an artist as well.

Ophelia.

He closed his eyes and tried not to think about the woman he'd lost. No, not lost. She'd taken her own life after they'd parted ways.

Shadows of the Past

It hadn't been his fault, yet the guilt and memories remained behind. He rubbed his temples. This wasn't the time or the place to deal with this. He had to focus on keeping Lily safe. Which meant it was time to stop wallowing in self-pity and get on with his work.

Michael opened his eyes and sighed. It took another couple of minutes before he knew he could focus. Michael took a small flashlight from his pocket and walked the backyard. He examined the fence step by step, each board and connection to the fence frame. No new footsteps, nothing that suggested anyone had been in the yard except himself and Lily. Odd. He'd known the police had checked the yard, but there was no real sign of their presence.

Had someone been in the back and tidied up?

If so, how had they made their way back here without being seen?

Maybe the police hadn't walked the fence line?

It was possible except... He frowned and crouched down to scrutinize the ground.

Rake lines. If there'd been any footsteps here or anything else for that matter, it was all gone. Michael cursed under his breath and rose, looking around the yard. What else had he missed, and when had they been back here? Could it have been the police cleaning up after themselves, but it didn't fit what he knew. He'd never come across a cop who had cleaned up a scene or any signs of their investigation.

Richmond would know, and Michael could check in with the detective in the morning. The man would want to do a follow-up after the night's events. Michael had emailed the detective with copies of the photographs he'd taken of his minor injuries earlier in the day. He didn't have to wait until the morning to reach out to Richmond. He could shoot off a message before he called it a night.

With that in mind, Michael completed his circuit of the backyard and headed inside, locked the back door, and secured it with a chain. He did the same with the front door. He'd added the chains to both doors after John had left, which would add an extra layer of security to the house. It was one thing to have access to a key, another to get past a chain without creating additional noise.

It took him another twenty minutes to complete his check of the windows. Once it was done, he turned the lights off downstairs and made his way upstairs. He paused at the top of the stairs, his gaze drawn to Lily's room. Was she already in bed or still soaking in the tub?

He groaned at the thought of her skin glistening from the steam as she relaxed in the bubble-scented hot water.

Naked, wet, and tempting. Michael's cock thickened at the image, and before he'd realized it, he had taken a step toward her bedroom. His hands clenched into fists, and he focused on his breathing. He'd promised her space, time to think things through. He wasn't going to storm in on her no matter how badly he wanted to touch her, taste her, and join her in the bath.

Michael shook off the image and turned to go to his room. Tomorrow would be a long day. Lily still had a couple of appearances ahead of her, including the convention, and with Daniel no longer in the scene, Michael didn't know for certain exactly how it would all work out. Another thing to add to his list of items he'd need to talk to Harvey about when morning rolled around.

Shadows of the Past

Chapter Ten

Lily yawned, stretched out, and rolled onto her back as she nestled under the blankets. Sleep had been hard to find. The last time she'd checked the clock it had been four. Her mind refused to settle down and had thrown far too many questions her way as she'd done her best to rest.

Most of those questions had centered on Michael.

No surprise there.

Her skin tingled at the thought of the man. God, even after one night, twice in bed with him in the space of twenty-four hours, she missed him. Without thinking about it, Lily reached out across her bed in search of the body she knew wasn't there. She curled onto her side and looked at the empty half of the bed. Odd. She hadn't allowed him to enter her room, but she missed him, expected him to be there in her bed. It didn't make sense, and yet the pain and need vibrated through her.

How could she need a man she barely knew? Shit, she didn't know anything about him beyond the fact he worked in security and he was a Dom. No, there were a few other things. There'd been another woman in his life, and it hadn't ended well. Someone Michael didn't want to talk about, at least not with her. Was the other woman still around? Did he have contact with her? The way he'd reacted there was pain involved and not the type he liked to play with.

What had happened between them?

Lily sighed and glanced up at the ceiling. She hadn't bothered to turn on the bedside lamp, and her eyes had adjusted to the early-morning light that had filtered in through the curtains.

What time was it?

Not that it mattered; she had no real plans for the day, and the house was secured. It would be another day or two before the replacement window was in, and if Daniel had done his job, she had the time to take a breath or two for herself. Sure, she'd get some work done before the end of the day, but she had no desire to spend the entire time slogging her way through commissions.

The cell phone rang. Lily turned, reached out, and grabbed it from the side table. With a yawn, she accepted the call and pressed the phone to her ear. "Hello?"

"Lily, did I wake you up?" John's familiar voice carried through the phone.

"No, I was awake."

"Good, good." John's smile was apparent even through the phone. "I had a long chat with Daniel yesterday. Man, he was pissed. I don't know what happened between the two of you, but I've never seen him like that before."

Lily closed her eyes and kept her voice calm. "Is everything okay?"

"Yes and no. Daniel's handed off your files. He made me call all of your current commissions and tell them the due dates had been pushed back a week because of personal circumstances."

"Damnit, he was supposed to make those calls himself." Typical. Of course Daniel wasn't going to make the calls himself. She should have realized it when they'd spoken in the kitchen. "I'm sorry you had to do that for him, John."

"It's okay. I don't mind. There was only one who threw a fit, said she'd been promised it on time, and the woman was going to hold you to the contract. I passed her on to Daniel."

One problem. Okay, Lily could live with that and let people know Daniel had had no right to sign contracts in her name if things blew up. "Thank you, John."

He coughed, the sound echoing through the line. "What happened between the two of you? I really do need to know if I'm going to deal with your files."

"You might want to check with the others he's working with—if he's pulled the same thing with them as he has me. I mean, he didn't have the right to sign contracts in my name." She sighed and rested one hand over her eyes. "It's my own fault. I let it get to this point before I realized what was happening."

"Oh God, I had no idea, Lily. He signs for most of the people we work with. I assumed it was in your contract, but I didn't know how much work he had lined up for you this month." The rustle of papers being shuffled filtered down through the line. "I took a quick look at the lineup, and there's almost three months of work crammed into a thirty-day period. I don't know what he was thinking when he did this."

Nor did Lily. "Is he in the office right now?"

"No, he hasn't shown up yet. He was here late last night and in a foul mood. I doubt he went straight home. Not with the way he was acting."

Lily closed her eyes and took a deep breath. "How bad was it?"

"Things thrown around in his office, mugs, papers, you know the thing. Honestly, I've never seen him like this before, and I've known him for years now."

"Anyone hurt?" *Please, don't let it have gone that far.*

"No, nothing like that. Daniel was ranting about how you betrayed him, and how it's all Michael's fault. I don't know why he'd think that, but he was pretty vocal about it all. You and I should meet up in the next day or so and go over how you want to handle all of this. Get a contract worked out."

At least John understood they needed a new contract in place before anything else could happen. "Sounds like a good idea. I'll have a lawyer go over it before I sign it. Sorry, John. I just can't take any risks, not after what happened."

"No, no, I understand completely. I wouldn't want you to sign anything right now without legal advice." John soothed her concerns. "Daniel will be back in the office soon, and I don't think I want him overhearing anything we say right now. He's unpredictable, and it might backfire on both of us."

She tensed at the words. Backfire how? Did Daniel have something on her that could ruin her career? She frowned and tried to think of anything he might have, but she drew a blank. Her life wasn't squeaky clean, but it was at least honest. To her knowledge, she'd never broken the law. There weren't any pictures out there of her doing anything she was ashamed of, and since the appearance of the stalker, she'd been extra careful about her behavior. "Not sure what you mean."

There was a pause before John continued, his voice pitched low. "He has files on everyone, you, me, everyone he's ever worked with. I don't know what's in them as he has them in a locked cabinet, but it can't be good. I mean, we all have secrets we don't want to come out. I'm going to try to find out exactly what's in the files before I see you. Better we have all our ducks in a row, right?"

A band of tension formed across her chest as her breathing hitched. "Sure, right."

"I'll call you when I can. Talk to you later, Lily." The line went dead before she could say another word.

Lily stared at the phone. Secret files? What was going on? What exactly was Daniel doing? There wasn't anything he could have on her, was there? Unless Daniel had framed her for something? Would he have gone that far? Her stomach knotted, then growled.

God, whatever the man was up to, she needed to get her head clear so she could think.

Lily rolled off the bed, her bare feet hitting the floor as her stomach rumbled again.

When was the last time she'd eaten?

Toast yesterday, but nothing since. Lily frowned as she pulled on a robe and stuffed her feet into a pair of house shoes. She ran her hands through her hair and scowled. She needed to run a brush through the mess and do something about it before she ran into Michael. God, she couldn't let him see her like this.

Why not? If there's to be a chance between us, he has to see me in all my morning glory.

She chuckled at the image but still grabbed her brush, sat on the edge of the bed, and worked it through her hair. Each new knot

Shadows of the Past

she hit triggered a wince as she smoothed out the tangles. Food. They'd both need something to eat, but the thought of entering the kitchen, the scene of a fight she didn't want to think about, sickened her. No, if there was ever a time to hit a restaurant for breakfast, it was today.

Now all she had to do was persuade Michael.

* * * *

Michael eased into the booth as Lily settled in on the opposite side of the table. Breakfast out had been an excellent idea. After everything that had happened the day before, they both needed a break from the house, and returning to the coffee shop hadn't appealed to either of them. Fortunately, Lily had suggested a local diner, and the smells that welcomed him when they walked in through the front door told him Lily had made a decent choice.

"I don't eat here on a daily basis, but it's always been a welcoming place. The food is great, service is decent, and they don't hurry you away from the table." Lily glanced up from the menus after the server slipped away to get their drinks.

At least he hadn't fallen into the trap of *do you come here often?* "Looks like a decent place, and it was a good suggestion. Eating out, I mean."

She glanced back at the menu. "I couldn't face walking into the kitchen, not after the fight with Daniel." Her shoulders tensed, knuckles white as she spoke.

God, he hated seeing Lily hurting like this. It was one thing to turn a woman over his lap and spank her or take a paddle to her backside. It was another to cause her emotional pain. "I know it hurts when you're betrayed by someone you believed to be your friend."

Lily set the menu down, and the conversation paused when the server brought their drinks, took their orders, and moved away.

"You don't have to talk about it if you don't want to. I'm not here to push you into anything, Lily." Except for into his bed, if he could, but even then, persuade would be closer to the mark than push. Force wasn't his thing, would never be his thing, except in a scene they'd already agreed to. "If all you want to do is sit and have breakfast, that's fine by me." Any time with her was welcome. Hell, he didn't want to think about leaving her, not now, not until the stalker was dealt with.

She sighed and rubbed the back of her neck. "It's been a lot of stress of late."

"I can understand."

"I trusted Daniel. Not only short term but for years. It doesn't make sense to me. Why would he ever do something like that to me? To anyone?" Lily leaned back against the booth. "Daniel was there when I needed him, but over the last year he's changed." She caught her bottom lip between her teeth.

His hand itched with the need to reach out and touch her. She needed comfort, protection, and a friend to tell her it would be all right. "You don't have to go through this alone, Lily."

"I'm not alone." She lifted her gaze, a nervous smile touching her lips. "You're with me. I know you're not going to turn around and walk away. Not while all this is going on, at least."

He didn't know what to say, but his heart skipped a beat even as his blood raced to his cock. Thankfully he wouldn't have to stand up anytime soon. "I'm here for you, Lily. Whatever happens, I'll be right here for you." He kept his voice calm and warm.

"I don't know what to think about this situation between us, Michael." Lily licked her bottom lip. "What we did the other day, then the way you held me through the night—it was special, but I don't know what we are. If there is an *us* or this is something else. Stress related, maybe?"

Is that what she thought it was? Nothing more than a way to ease stress in a tense situation? "No, it's not about that. I wanted you. I still want you."

"We need to be honest with each other. You already know far more about me than I know about you, and that needs to change." She turned away for a moment, her gaze tracking the movement of the servers through the diner. "You're a Dominant?"

"Yes."

"And there have been others in your life." It wasn't a question.

"Yes." Where was she going with this?

"Mostly casual?" She arched an eyebrow.

His gut knotted. "All but one." *Am I ready for this conversation?* Maybe it was time to make himself talk about it.

"It didn't end nicely, did it?"

"Ended well enough. It's what happened after it all ended that caused the real problems for me." His throat tightened. "It's not a situation I talk about. Only a few people know what happened." Harvey and a couple of the guys he worked with. Sure, plenty knew the basics but not the gory details. Those he'd kept to himself. "I'm not sure you want to hear this."

"I think I need to understand it if we're going to have a chance."

"Fair point." He leaned back. "I believe we should wait until our food arrives though." It wasn't a topic he wanted to discuss around the server. Fortunately, the diner was quiet enough right then that no one else was sitting close enough to them to be able to overhear their conversation.

Lily glanced up and twisted in her seat so she could see the counter, a tender smile on her lips when she turned back to meet his gaze. "Perhaps you're right."

They fell into a comfortable silence as they waited, which gave him the time to go over what he had to share with Lily. Memories threatened to flood his mind, and he tried to sort through them. It wasn't going to be easy, and the conversation might mean the end of their relationship, but she deserved the truth.

Could you call what had formed between them a relationship? It wasn't as though he'd said he loved her, though he'd implied those feelings were there. Still, women liked to hear the word. *Not only women.* Fine, okay, he wanted to hear the word from Lily, but it was too soon to expect a declaration and believe it. Hell, he didn't know if he'd understand why she would say it when they barely knew each other.

The server returned five minutes later and set their meals down. After checking on their drinks, she left them to it. As usual, Michael had taken a seat with his back to the wall where he could watch the door and anyone approaching them without a problem.

"Looks appetizing."

"I've never had any problems with the food here." Lily dug into her omelet and gestured to his plate. "I've had their hash brown and scramble mix before. Always turned out delicious."

He had no arguments, especially after the first bite. The next few minutes were filled with the silence of them eating, disturbed only by the server checking to see if everything was all right with their meals.

Michael waited for the woman to leave, took a bite, and gave himself a moment to form his words. "Her name was Olivia."

Lily met his gaze and nodded to indicate she had heard him.

"I was young. Nineteen when we got together, and twenty when it ended." Far too young for what Ophelia had wanted. "I was new to the lifestyle. Shit, I'd played around, read a few books, and I knew what I wanted in life. I'd had a couple of brief encounters. One with a much older woman who taught me a little more about this type of thing, and it answered questions about who I was."

Lily arched an eyebrow at the mention of an older woman, but she didn't push.

"Ophelia was drawn to being a submissive. She was, like you, an artist, but she was weaker. No, being honest, she couldn't stand up for herself, and I think she was searching for a protector of sorts. One who could take over her life." He was getting ahead of himself. He paused to eat a few bites, then drink, buying time.

"I've met people like that, men and women who are always on the lookout for someone to take care of them." She frowned and set her glass down. "Isn't that how most submissives are?"

Michael shook his head and smiled. "No, nothing like that. Most are very strong-willed and able to look after themselves. Many

Shadows of the Past

work. Some own a business or are in high-pressure, powerful positions careerwise. They choose to submit to one or more people in their lives, but it's not because they are weak. In fact, more than a few of the submissives I've known have been among the strongest men and women I've ever had the pleasure of knowing. No, Ophelia wasn't just submissive; she was needy. She didn't want to do anything without being told to, ordered to. She took TPE—total power exchange—to an entirely new level. Hell, even if all she wanted was a TPE relationship, it would have been too much for me. I wasn't ready to control someone to that level, and I don't think I ever would be." How much should he tell her? The truth, the entire truth. It was the only way to make sure she understood what had happened.

"What exactly did she want?" Lily pressed, her gaze fixed on his face.

"It started out okay between us. We moved in together after about three months. Then it began to build up. I was working and going to college, my time was limited, but Ophelia wanted me to give her rules that would govern every part of her life. I tried. It was exciting at first, but it became difficult. The more I gave, the more she wanted." Ophelia, sweet, beautiful Ophelia. God, she'd been all he'd wanted back then. Submissive, sexually willing, and eager to please him. It should have been perfect. "It stopped being fun, it was work, and she still wasn't happy with it all."

"Work?"

"People think being a Dominant is all fun and games, but even if it never steps out of the bedroom, there's a commitment the Dominant makes to taking care of the submissive. She, or he, is theirs to protect and watch over. It's part of what makes the bond between them so real. A lot of the time, it boils down to making sure the submissive takes care of themselves. A gentle reminder here and there when the submissive is working too hard or forgets to do something important, a task they've agreed to take care of."

God, he'd been an idiot thinking he was ready for a relationship like that, but the idea had been appealing at the time. Now that he knew better, it wasn't what he wanted.

Dominating a woman in the bedroom, the occasional intense scene at a club, those he could enjoy. But controlling each minute of every day in the life of his submissive? No. Been there, done that, never again.

Not even with the right person?

No, the last time had all but destroyed him. The fun had gone out of it before it had even begun.

"She wanted that?"

"In ways you might find hard to believe. It got to the point where Ophelia wouldn't do anything, not even use the bathroom, without permission from me." He turned his attention to the remains of his meal. Odd. He couldn't remember eating most of it.

"The bathroom?" Lily blinked, her eyes wide with shock. "People actually do that?"

"Some do, and for some, it works. Most, I think, set up rules to govern the life of their submissive, though in those cases they prefer the term *slave*, but it wasn't for me. I had nothing left outside of work, school, and giving her orders. Even sex became a chore." Had he ever thought sex would be nothing more than work to him, especially at such a young age? "I couldn't bring myself to come home most nights, and I stayed at a friend's, which only led to arguments."

Lily's gaze softened. "Did she realize there was a problem?"

It had been one of the hardest things about the situation. "If Ophelia did, she didn't tell me. She didn't say anything she believed might displease me. She'd lost the ability to stand up to anyone at all, even if it meant she ended up hurt." Ophelia had done that only once, and it had been the final straw. "I tried to make it work, but when it began to destroy me, I finally realized I had to put an end to it. I stopped the TPE, but she still acted as if it existed, refused to back down from being mine in all ways. I had no choice left if I wanted to keep my sanity, and I broke things off. I moved out. It was the only thing I could do to end it between us, since she wouldn't stop."

Lily reached out with one hand and touched his. "It doesn't end there, does it?"

Had there been something in his voice? "No, it doesn't." His throat tightened, and he swallowed past a lump he hadn't known existed until that moment. "I refused to answer her letters, kept away from the apartment, and made what I thought was a clean break of it. I didn't know what else to do as she'd refused to accept that things had changed between us. I'd loved her once and still cared for her, but it had to be over between us for my own sanity."

Lily stroked the back of his hand, her touch gentle. "Then what?"

"It had been three months. I'd focused on my work and school. No dating. I'd been burned and didn't want to jump back into anything when I knew I wasn't ready." The need had still been there, but he'd learned to control it. "Then I found out she was dead." He'd been in class; there'd been a newspaper on the professor's desk. Ophelia's name and photograph there for the world to see.

Shit, he shouldn't have found out that way. No one should have, but it hadn't been the end of it. "She'd committed suicide. I didn't understand what had happened, why she'd done it, but I didn't get the chance to remain ignorant."

"What happened?" Lily picked up his hand and covered it with her own. "Let it all out."

Yes, he needed to, not only because Lily had the right to know, but because he needed to talk about Ophelia. "There was a letter. I'd moved into a shared apartment, which is likely all that saved me from doing something stupid."

"A letter from Ophelia?" she pressed, her hand firm as she held his.

"Yes. Ophelia blamed me for her actions. For leaving her, for not doing what she needed me to do. Ophelia claimed she couldn't function without me there, controlling her, being there for her every step of the way. She laid it out in crisp, precise detail." He closed his eyes, not wanting to look at Lily, not when all he could see was Ophelia. "I didn't do that. I didn't abandon her. I tried to get her to back off and work with me to make things easier for us. I wasn't ready for what she wanted. Shit, I don't think I'd ever be ready for what she wanted me to do." He forced himself to open his eyes again. "God, I didn't get involved in any form of kink for years. I even tried going vanilla, but it wasn't me."

Vanilla. Michael had shut himself down and almost made the worst mistake of his life by sleeping with the wrong woman after he'd ended it with Ophelia. One who expected him to settle down, have kids, and do the white picket fence thing. As soon as he'd realized what was happening, he'd broken it off and got the hell out of Dodge. Fuck, it had been a casual thing between them to begin with, but the woman had other ideas.

"And now?" Lily eased her grip on him.

"I can't hide who I am, so I stopped trying. I found a club, and I play on occasions. Nothing serious. I keep myself safe, apart from complications, but things have changed." Michael pulled back from her touch and ran his hands through his hair. "There you have it. I'm damaged goods, Lily. Broken, but with you? God, I don't know, but I feel whole again." *Stupid, stupid, stupid. She isn't ready to hear that.* "I'm not promising anything because I can't right now. I just know how I am around you, how I want to be with you. I know it's dangerous because you're new to all of this, and I'm working, supposed to be protecting you." He wanted to say more, so much more, but his phone rang, and he eased it from his pocket and glanced at the display.

Work.

"I'll be right back. I need to take this." He offered a smile of an apology and slipped out of the booth. Lily needed time to digest the information he'd given her, and maybe this call would allow her the chance to think things through.

LILY FELL SILENT as Michael walked out of the diner, his cell phone pressed to his ear. He hadn't needed to leave to take the call.

Shadows of the Past

They'd both known that, yet he'd done it regardless. She nibbled on her bottom lip and tried to stay calm. Why had he left?

To give her time to think?

Well, sure, she had a lot to go over. The story, the way he'd explained what had happened when he'd been a teenager, had been painful for him to share. Still, he'd managed it. He'd trusted her enough to share his past.

Lily glanced down at her now-empty plate. They couldn't stay here for the rest of the day. Sooner or later, they'd have to return to her house. If she kept avoiding the kitchen, then she'd let Daniel win, and it was bad enough the stalker had caused so many problems for her in the past couple of months. She wasn't about to let her one-time manager upset her life.

"Is everything all right?" The server moved to the side of the booth. "You look a little off. An argument with your boyfriend?"

Lily forced a smile. "He's not my boyfriend."

The server turned toward the door. "Oh, he's single?"

No, he's mine. "I don't think so." Lily tried to keep the heat from her words. "A man like him is seldom single."

"Yeah, you're right. Still, you can't blame a girl for hoping." The server sighed. "Damn, he's a natural nine. Would be a ten if it weren't for those scars."

Lily scowled. There was nothing wrong with his scars. They were a part of him, part of what made him special. "I don't know. I think they add to who he is. A unique touch."

"Yeah, I guess." The server shook her head. "Can I get you anything else?"

"Not yet. I'll know more when he comes back from his call."

"If he comes back in. You never know with a guy like that. He might leave and stiff you with the bill." The server grinned. "No, you're right. He's not the type to eat and run." The server cleared up a few things and made her way back to the counter, checking on her other customers along the way.

Lily sighed and leaned back in the booth and closed her eyes.

Michael wouldn't walk away from her, not unless she told him to. The real question was, did she want him to leave?

A band tightened around her heart at the idea of him walking away, of never seeing him again.

That answers that question.

The door chime alerted her to someone entering the diner, and she opened her eyes, a smile claiming her lips the moment she realized Michael had walked back in. Her breasts tightened and nipples tingled as she straightened up and pushed her shoulders back before she'd realized what she was doing. "You okay?"

"It was Harvey. He ran the prints on the note, but whoever it is isn't in the system." Michael slid back into the booth. "They've narrowed down the footprint to shoe type and size, and Harvey's going to talk to your detective and share what we have. Hopefully they found prints on the rock used to smash the window."

Forensics? Was that what it would boil down to? Outside of TV shows, she knew little or nothing about such things and would leave it to those who did. "The entire situation creeps me out." *Understatement of the year.* Whoever was behind all of this had no idea what they were doing to her or her life. Or maybe they did, which made matters all the worse.

"We'll get to the bottom of it, Lily."

She rubbed her temples. Was she ready to tell Michael what was going on? What she thought about the idea of him leaving? She ran the tip of her tongue over her bottom lip.

"I wish you wouldn't do that." Michael groaned.

"Do what?"

"Lick your lips, nibble on them, catch them between your teeth." He shifted in the booth.

"Why?" She leaned forward. Was he squirming? Something bubbled into life within her chest. A sense of pride and pleasure at his actions. Control, power. Was this like being a Dominant? No, she didn't feel Dominant. Instead, she felt strong, sensual, and ready to tease him a little more.

Shadows of the Past

"It makes me want to see what else you can do with those lips."

"Maybe we should find out." Had she actually spoken out loud?

"Lily, don't tease me. Not if you're going to walk away from me when this case is over."

She couldn't help but frown. "I'm not the one who would walk away, Michael."

His smile lit up the room. "Is that how you feel?"

"Yes."

He reached out across the table and took her hand, lifting it to his lips before he placed a tender, sensual kiss on the backs of her knuckles. Lily shivered as a wave of heat washed over her. She pressed her thighs together and tried not to squirm. All she could think about was the time they'd shared in his bed.

His bed, not hers.

He'd bared his heart to her, and perhaps it was time she did the same thing—let down the walls and allow him into her bed. Her room. The one place where no man had been allowed. She met his gaze. All she could do was imagine herself in his arms once more. "I need you."

"*Need* is a compelling word." His voice was low and husky.

"Yes, it is," she agreed. Was she blushing? She could feel the heat radiating across her cheeks. "If you're not ready to hear it, I understand."

"I could stand to hear a lot more, but I'm not going to push." Michael rubbed his thumb across the backs of her knuckles. "I want more with you, so much more, Lily. But I also need to get a few details cleared up. What we have done is only the beginning. If we take this step, it's going to be the start of a deeper relationship between us. I have to let the Dominant out with you, but I will take it slow. It won't be something rushed for you, for us, but the dominance will increase."

"Only in the bedroom though." Her mouth dried out.

"Yes, only in the bedroom."

Chapter Eleven

Michael closed the passenger-side door and walked around to the driver's side before he got in. She hadn't run away from him, hadn't pulled away. Even when he'd revealed his past with Ophelia, Lily hadn't withdrawn from him.

Did she feel sorry for him? Was that why she'd remained with him?

No, it wouldn't explain her sexual reaction to him, and there was no denying the way she'd squirmed in the booth when he'd warned her what playing with her bottom lip had done to him. Had she blushed? There'd been a small reaction, but he'd been focused on the way she had moved. He smiled at the memory. *Little minx.*

"Home then?" Lily asked.

"Yes, I think it's for the best." Though making love to her in the car held an appeal of its own, not with the stalker around. "We need time and space for what I have in mind."

The chair squeaked as she shifted in the seat next to him. "I don't know if I'm going to be able to do all the things you want, but I'll try."

He reached across the car and gently touched her cheek. "I know you will, my Lily. You're going to be fine. Whatever we do, you will be wonderful. You're all I've ever wanted in life."

"Thank you." Her voice was husky. "I want to believe that."

"You will be all right. Trust me on this." What they had planned to share was enough to make any newcomer more than a touch unsteady. "You have your safe word system. Remember the traffic lights?"

"Yes." The single word was barely more than a whimper.

His cock twitched at her reaction. His hands tightened on the steering wheel, knuckles white as he struggled to keep his focus. He had to do it, had to get them back to Lily's house before he lost what control he had left and pulled off to the side of the road.

Shadows of the Past

Damn it all, how could he be like this? His body wasn't his own when it came to Lily. How did she do this to him?

It didn't matter. His body knew who and what he wanted.

"You might regret doing this," Lily suggested.

Michael glanced in the rearview mirror. The road wasn't overly busy, but there were a few other vehicles behind them. "I doubt it. I can't imagine ever regretting any time spent with you." Three cars, one black, one blue, one white. Anything else was too far back for him to be able to get a decent read on the situation.

"Something wrong?"

"No, just keeping an eye on the traffic." Did he have enough toys to be able to work with Lily? He certainly hadn't brought anything with him, but he had a couple of belts, his hands, and his mind. There were always other things he could use, and after all, a good Dominant only truly needed his mind, or so he'd been told. Well, now he would get the chance to put his abilities to the test.

Lily fell silent as they drove, and the occasional glance confirmed she appeared to be lost in thought. He couldn't blame her. She had a lot to think about after their conversation, and he could only hope she wasn't about to change her mind. Still, if she did, he'd respect her choice. He'd always respect her right to say no or not now. He couldn't imagine doing anything else, even if he, like many Dominants, held darker fantasies buried in the back of his mind. But with this woman, with Lily, he wouldn't let the darkness out.

He had never let it out.

Michael rechecked the mirror as he readied for a turn. Two of the same cars remained in his rearview mirror, but the other had vanished. No doubt it had turned off at some point or parked. The road was a busy one, and it wasn't unusual for there to be the appearance of being followed, yet something didn't quite sit right with the blue car.

Minnesota plates, which wasn't unusual, but the car was new, a small SUV. Another glance confirmed the make. The driver was male, but other than that the car was too far back to make out any details about the driver beyond the fact he was white with short hair.

Five minutes later, the blue car finally peeled off behind them, and Michael relaxed.

If that's the stalker, he knows where Lily lives. He won't need to follow us all the way back, only enough to be certain of where we were going.

Just because the driver had come close to her home, it didn't mean it was the stalker. Still, Michael would be on the lookout for the blue SUV again. Had there been a bike rack on the car? There'd been an attachment on the back, but he hadn't had enough time to confirm it, not with the traffic around them. When they got to the house, he'd do a full check to make sure the property was still secure before they took any time for themselves. That way he'd be able to relax with Lily and give her the attention she deserved.

"You seem tense."

"I thought I saw something, but it was nothing." Michael flashed Lily a smile. He wasn't exactly lying; the car had turned off, and there was no longer anything to worry her about. He pulled the car into the drive and turned off the engine. "Are you sure about this?"

"Yes." She unbuckled and turned in the seat, her eyes soft as she met his gaze. "I've never been so sure about anything in my life."

* * * *

He punched the steering wheel, his hands clenched into fists as he sat in the parking spot. The diner. Of all the places she could have taken Michael, she had to take him to that damned diner. The one place that had been theirs. Hadn't he met her there? He scowled and leaned back in his chair and closed his eyes. When had they met? Fuck it. He knew the memories were there. He could recall every time they'd met, spoke, what they'd talked about, but now his memories were jumbled.

Breathe, calm, and focus. That was all he had to do to bring himself back under control.

Shadows of the Past

There, he could remember now. Lily had been at the counter paying the bill, and he'd walked in. She'd been dressed simply in a flowing summer dress, her hair up in a ponytail, face fresh-scrubbed without the slightest hint of makeup. Young and honest. She'd smiled at him, and in their shared moment, he'd known what was between them, what would always exist, no matter who tried to get in the way.

That was what it was. Michael must have known the place was special to her and insisted they go there for a meal. It was his fault, but Lily should have stood up to him. Lily would have to be punished for her mistake, her weakness.

Yes, she'd beg for forgiveness, then promise never to let anyone else touch her again. His cock twitched at the thought, the way her body would welcome him and only him. He had their place arranged, away from it all where she could practice her art, but again it would be only for him. She'd no longer have to whore her work out the way she now did. He would take care of her until the end of their days together.

That was what she wanted. What she needed. Someone to protect her, teach her, and guide her. No one else knew her the way he did, and when Michael was out of the way...

No, he wouldn't wait for the man to leave.

He would take her.

Soon.

* * * *

Lily's heart raced. The drive back to her house had given her far too much time to think about what Michael had in mind. Images flashed through her thoughts, all of them kinky, but it didn't mean they would become a reality. If she knew nothing else about the man, he was careful. Yes, he was Dominant, or at least he was from what she'd experienced with him so far, but he wasn't hardcore.

Or was he?

Had he hidden it from her?

He'd been gentle; he'd been honest about who he was, and her skin tingled with the possibilities that lay ahead.

This was a man she was comfortable with. Her body craved him, and she was at peace with him in a way she had never experienced before. Men often came on either too hard or too soft. They pushed too much or didn't push at all and hung around the fringes of her life, vanishing before she was even aware if they had an interest in her. Not Michael. He'd been honest, teasing her from the start. There'd been the threat of a spanking when she'd laughed at him that morning in her backyard. Damn, her body had reacted to his suggestion.

Had he known how she responded when she was around him?

He'd been watching her closely. He was fascinated with what she might do with her mouth. Did it mean he'd want her to give him a blowjob? Cold sweat coated her palms. He wouldn't be pleased with her if she had to do that, but she'd try. She didn't have much experience there, nor was she any good at it, at least according to the one man she'd tried to please that way.

The memory of the harsh words that had been thrown at her resurfaced.

"Stupid cunt, can't even blow a man. What use are you?"

There'd been more, so much more, but she tried to shut it out.

Now she stood at the bottom of her steps and struggled to keep her fears under control. Michael wouldn't say that to her, wouldn't degrade her. Michael had already told her humiliation wasn't his thing. She had to believe him. Had to cling to the idea he would never hurt her. He'd told her what to say to end a scene, and she had nothing to indicate he would break his rules.

Michael moved behind her and wrapped his arms around her waist as he pulled her in against his chest. "You have nothing to fear from me, Lily."

She closed her eyes and leaned in. "I know. I'm being silly."

"No, you're not. Now, where do you want to spend our time together?" He nuzzled the side of her neck.

She shivered; heat rippled through her body as the tension

eased from her limbs. "I can do this, but use my bedroom this time."

"Are you sure?"

Did he understand what she was offering to him? "Yes, I am."

"All right. Go upstairs, undress, and kneel at the foot of your bed, thighs spread, hands locked behind your back, head bowed." He released his grip on her waist. "Remember your safe words, how to stop, and what to say when I check in with you." He tapped her backside with a sharp snap, enough to send a jolt through her body but not enough to truly hurt.

Lily yelped and darted up the stairs before she realized what she was doing. The orders weren't something she'd expected outside the bedroom, but the idea heated her inner walls. Her body craved his touch; she wanted him more than she was willing to admit even to herself.

She stopped in front of her bedroom. Was she doing the right thing? Yes, of course she was. She took a deep breath and walked into her room. Everything was exactly the way she'd left it, including her unmade bed. She couldn't let him see it like this. Lily tugged the bedding back into place, straightening it up before she turned and looked at the door.

How long did she have before he would follow her?

Lily tugged off her clothing, setting it to one side, folded neatly. With that out of the way, she settled onto her knees at the foot of her bed and parted her thighs. Heat flushed across her cheeks as she crossed her wrists behind her back. She'd never felt so exposed in her life, but he wanted this, and she wanted to give it to him. As she heard footsteps, she lowered her head and fixed her gaze on the thick carpet.

The door opened, then closed a moment later as Michael entered the room. Lily fought the urge to look up.

"Nicely done," Michael commented as he moved to her side. "Don't break position."

"Yes, Sir."

He brushed his fingers over her shoulder. "You remembered.

Excellent."

She shivered beneath his caress and struggled to hold position when all she wanted to do was lean in to his touch and relax.

Michael pressed his fingers beneath her chin and lifted her gaze. "You have no idea how beautiful you look like this, Lily."

Warmth claimed her as she looked into his eyes. "Thank you, Sir." She wanted to disagree with him, but instinct said it wouldn't go down well with Michael.

"You wanted to argue with me, didn't you?" His grip tightened on her chin.

"Yes, Sir."

"It's something we can work on in time, but I want to focus on pleasure right now." He moved back a step and reached for his jeans. "We'll start with my pleasure. I've been fantasizing about your lips on and off since we met, and the incident in the diner only added to my desires."

Lily felt the blood drain from her face. The one thing she had hoped to avoid, and it was the first thing he wanted to do with her tonight. She looked away from him and struggled to bring her fears under control.

"What's wrong, my Lily?"

"You want me to do something I'm terrible at, Sir," she admitted. What was she going to do now? He'd find out she wasn't the woman he wanted. After all, didn't all men want a woman who could deep-throat them and be perfect when it came to blowjobs? Oh God, he'd tell her to leave once he found out how horrible she was.

"Let me decide that for myself, and if you need to learn, then I'll help you."

No, then Michael would decide it was over, or he'd be cruel and hurtful in his rejection of her. *He's not like that. He isn't the type to strike out at me.* "Yes, sir."

"Keep your hands behind your back." He brushed his fingertips over her cheek. "And look at me."

Shadows of the Past

She obeyed, though her stomach knotted. She could do this; even if things between them blew up on her, she could do it. Lily watched him as he undid his jeans and slipped his erect cock free from its confines. Her breath caught as she looked at him, his erection in front of her face. It was thick and long. She'd already known that from their night together, but being on her knees gave her an entirely new viewpoint in more ways than one.

"Take a long look at it. You need to know my body just as I will know yours. Each detail and flaw, where I like to be touched, and what I don't like. I'll be doing the same with you."

Why does it mean I need to give you a blowjob?

"Open your mouth."

Fear bubbled through Lily, but she obeyed slowly. Her lips parted only a touch at first, but she knew what was expected and opened them wide enough to accept the head of his cock, expecting him to ram into her mouth. She'd choke—there was no denying it—and then he'd be angry with her or at least upset. She watched as he brought his cock closer. The engorged purple head brushed her lips, and she struggled to keep her mouth open. She had to try. Maybe he wouldn't be as disappointed with her if she showed she was trying?

"Don't move," Michael warned.

Lily didn't respond; she couldn't with the position she had been ordered into. Speech wasn't an option. Neither could she nod to show she had understood his order. Instead, Lily held position as he rubbed the head of his erection gently over her bottom lip. She inhaled as his scent surrounded her. Strong, musky, and so damned tempting. She didn't understand it. Why would she be drawn to his scent when the closeness of a cock to her mouth had, until this time, filled her with a mix of fear and disgust?

He eased the tip of his cock past her bottom lip and onto her tongue. No more than the head, giving her little more than a brief taste and feel of it before he drew back. God, she wanted more. She watched the way his thick erection jerked in front of her; a small bead of precum glistened on the slit, and Lily fought against the urge to lean forward and lick it clean.

"Now, take one hand and close it around the base of my cock."

Lily blinked, the order unexpected. "Yes, Sir." Was she allowed to speak now? It didn't matter. She'd already responded to him, and if she wasn't allowed to answer, he'd tell her or correct her as he had with the spanks the first time around. She grasped the base of his cock with her right hand, the touch timid at first as she looked up at him.

"Stroke me and use your tongue to explore me. You don't have to take me into your mouth right now, but get used to the feel of me beneath your tongue."

It was an odd request, at least to Lily, but she was willing to try. He wasn't about to shove himself into her mouth, which eased some of her concerns, and she breathed easily with the under-standing. Gingerly at first, she brushed her hand up the length of his cock, and he groaned in pleasure. Her touch, she knew, was gentle, not the firm grip that would be needed to please him entirely, but he didn't seem to have a complaint about what she was currently doing. His cock was close to her lips, and now all she had to do was lean forward to touch the tip of her tongue against the head.

His erection jerked and twitched in front of her.

Had she done that to him, the same way she'd caused him to groan from her touch?

She tightened her grip on his erection and stroked him as she traced the length of his cock with the tip of her tongue before she returned to lick the head. She paused for a moment and looked at the glistening drop of precum before she swiped it free and tasted him. Now it was her turn to groan, and her eyes half closed. She couldn't remember if she'd tasted something like this the last and only time she'd attempted this with a man, but she didn't think so.

"Let your instincts guide you, Lily."

She was being given free rein? She glanced up at Michael, and when he nodded his encouragement, she turned her attention back to his throbbing erection as it pulsed in her grip. She could do this. So far, she hadn't done anything wrong, and she would continue until he told her to stop. Trust. It was something she could give him just as he was trusting her not to hurt him. And she could, very easily, harm him. A scrape or closing of teeth at the wrong time was all it would take.

Lily closed her lips around his cock and closed her eyes. His taste filled her senses as she traced her tongue around his flesh. Her hand moved without thought as she squeezed and teased him; her free hand now nestled against his sac. She cupped his balls, the pressure light and gentle as she rolled the firm globes between her fingers. They were tight, and he trembled beneath her touch.

She was doing this to him. Her touch caused him to groan and quiver, and with that knowledge, her sense of power increased. It didn't make sense. He was the one in control. His commands told her what to do, yet she couldn't deny the power she experienced in this moment of submission, and it urged her on. With growing confidence, she sucked on the swollen head of his cock as she teased him with her tongue. With each new tug, she felt him respond and tasted his growing desire. His balls moved beneath her fingers, and his cock shuddered. He was getting close, and still, she continued.

"God, take a little more, my Lily. Please, a bit more." He slid one hand into her hair but didn't grasp it, his touch both firm and comforting.

She eased her lips down over his shaft but didn't push herself. An inch at a time, his cock filled her mouth though she wasn't ready to try to take all of him. Not yet, maybe not ever, but he didn't force the issue. Instead, he encouraged, stroked her hair and the side of her face. His sounds of bliss added to her confidence.

"So damn good." Michael's voice was ragged, his breathing hard.

A bit more. She could take him in and push his control. That was where her thoughts now focused: the need, the drive to push him over the edge and into the chasm of pleasure. She edged down on his cock and picked up the pace with her grip around him, teasing him as she worked his erection. All she knew right now was his taste, his cock, and his pleasure.

Her world shrank down to one thing: his erection. She couldn't think about anything else as she took him into her mouth again and again. Heat rippled between her thighs, but she was barely aware of it as she licked and sucked, her hand tight around his penis as she continued to work on him. He was close. She could feel it in the way he reacted to her; the pulse vibrated through her connection to him and his cock.

"Can't hold back. Lily, I'm going to come if you keep this up."

She wanted him to lose control, to come in her mouth and let her know she held power over him. She sucked all the harder. Pressure, friction, and the manipulation of his sac all added to the torment she was inflicting on Michael.

"Lily," Michael groaned a warning, his hand fisting in her hair. "God."

She wasn't going to stop. No matter what, she wasn't going to stop. She could do this, wanted to do this, even though a part of her screamed in fear. *Can I swallow if he comes?* There was only one way to find out. She didn't stop, didn't give up on what she was doing. Lily took him deeper, pushed past her fears until Michael filled her mouth completely. She couldn't take him down her throat. She had no idea how to even try, but this careful torment with lips and tongue—this she could do.

"Lily, final warning." The words were gasps as he began to thrust in and out of her mouth, never pushing any farther than she allowed.

One more push. That was all she had to do, a touch which would send him over the edge. She moaned around his cock, her tongue pressed to the underside of his erection.

"God!" he cried out, his cock pulsing as his orgasm hit.

Hot, wet jets of thick seed filled her mouth, and she swallowed it down. Pride and desire mingled in her core as she took him, knowing it was her touch, her tongue, and her mouth that had brought him to this point. She'd given him her submission, and in offering it, she had found her power.

Chapter Twelve

Michael's knees threatened to give out when he pulled his semi-hard cock free from Lily's lips and stared down at the still-kneeling and naked form of the woman he wanted to gather up into his arms. No woman had ever forced him to lose control. God, it wasn't like he hadn't had plenty of blowjobs in his life, but he'd always been in control, able to keep calm and say when or if he would come in their mouth. It had been his choice and his alone, but not this time. Somehow this all-too-innocent young woman had stripped his control away from him.

Focus. She still hasn't gained any pleasure for herself.

Or had she? He let his gaze move on her face; swollen lips, eyes wide and glossy, and her ragged breathing told him she was well and truly aroused. She'd enjoyed what she'd done, but it didn't mean he could zip up and walk out. No way in hell was he going to leave his Lily wanting.

"Onto the bed, hands and knees, head toward the headboard." Michael stepped out of his shoes.

Lily blinked once as if she hadn't realized she was still on her knees before she licked her bottom lip. His cock twitched at the memory of her tongue. She'd been a novice at that. Her nerves and then her growing desire to please him had all told him she'd had little or no experience with oral sex before tonight.

Lily crawled on her hands and knees to the bed, and he bit back a fresh groan at the sight of her naked ass. He hadn't told her to crawl. She'd done it of her own free will. A sign she wanted to please him? Yes, it was what his instincts told him. She was reveling in her sexuality and the way she'd made him react. He couldn't help but smile at the way she moved, the power in her newly awoken sexual desire, and he wasn't about to put her down. Not now, not anytime soon. That wasn't his style.

The bed creaked as she made her way up onto it and settled on her hands and knees; her still-braided hair hung over her shoulder as she glanced back at him. It took every ounce of his self-control not to pounce her, although he'd already come once between those full, sweet lips of hers.

He turned his back on her and brought himself under control as he stripped out of the rest of his clothes. Only then did he pick up the small bag he'd brought into the room with him. His cock twitched, ready to retake her, but he wasn't going to jump on her and bury himself between her thighs. No, she deserved far more. He'd give her the time to find herself, to submit to him fully.

Naked and in control once more, Michael moved to the head of the bed and brought three pillows to press beneath her belly to support her. "Stretch your hands out above your head." He reached down into the bag and brought out two belts, the only two he had with him, but he could work with it. He waited until Lily obeyed him before he used one belt to bind her wrists, making sure there was enough room between the belt and her wrists to allow blood flow but still give her the feeling of being restrained. The second belt he used to connect her now bound wrists to the headboard.

"Checking in with you, Lily. How are you?"

"Green," she whispered, her breathing faster than he had expected.

"Good." He checked the bindings and moved down the bed, his gaze lingering on her naked form. Beautiful. There was no other way of describing how she appeared to him. Soft, submissive, and willing, bound for his pleasure and hers. He traced the tips of his fingers down the length of her spine and watched her skin tighten beneath the passage of his touch. Small hairs rose along her back as he moved to her buttocks. Her muscles tensed beneath the circular pattern he made on her flesh, and she whimpered as she struggled to hold the position.

"You've no idea how tempting you are like this." He moved behind her and stopped. The twin tight globes of her ass drew his attention, and he rested one hand on her body. "You were always attractive to me, but this is something else. When I walked in earlier and saw you on your knees, I wanted to grab you and take you there and then. I'm still like that, but Dominants must remain in control of themselves. They can't dominate another if they fail to control themselves."

Lily whimpered and pressed into his touch. "I understand, Sir."

Did she? He could only hope that was the truth. If not, she would come to understand soon enough. "This body, at this moment, belongs to me, to do with as I wish unless you use your safe word." He couldn't tear his gaze away from her backside or the tempting mound between her thighs. "Part your legs a bit more, my Lily."

She complied, her back arching as she adjusted her position.

Her lower lips tempted him, but he didn't touch her, not immediately. Instead, he took a step back and moved around the bed to grab the small bag. Before he did anything else, he pulled out a tie and bound it around her eyes, stealing her sight. "With this in place, you will be able to focus more on sensations instead of what you would otherwise be able to see." He double-checked the belt around her wrists before he moved. He reached under Lily for a moment, cupping one breast, his thumb teasing her nipple and pinched it hard enough to steal a gasp from her lips.

"Sir," she whimpered as her hips rolled.

"Patience, sweetling." He squeezed her trapped breast before he moved away toward the bottom of the bed. He'd start slowly, build the fire within her core before he took her. He cupped and kneaded her buttocks, warming up her skin before he struck the first stinging slap against her skin. She jerked and tried not to make a sound, but he could hear the soft whimper she all but swallowed. "Don't hold back, Lily. Don't hide your reactions, the noises, the way your body wants to move. Unless I order you to silence or to remain still, you will not do so." He snapped out another slap. "You won't break position, but you can move on your hands and knees. Is that understood?"

"Yes, Sir."

Shadows of the Past

Michael smiled; he'd explained the basics, and she understood the check-in system. He could move on from here. He snapped four rapid blows against her ass and smiled. She jerked with each smack, a low sound marking the movement. Pink flushed across her backside, a color he intended to build upon. Michael shifted his position behind her and went from light snaps to firm smacks, first one cheek, then the other as heat claimed her flesh. She moaned, her head low, body reacting to the crack of his hand. Her hips rocked, and thighs parted a touch more, her nether lips swollen and coated with a liquid need he remembered all too well. It would have been easy to rush, but he refused to do so. Each new blow added to their arousal, and he paused only to massage her buttocks, ease the sting, and prevent her muscles from tightening. Once he was certain all was fine with Lily, Michael continued with the spanking until her breathing became ragged and his arm ached.

"Check in." He growled the word, one hand resting on her reddened buttocks. His cock ached, hard and erect as he looked at her. The room filled with the scent of her desire.

"Green, Sir," she whimpered.

"Good." Michael stepped back. He needed a moment to bring himself under control. "You're doing fine, my Lily. If we were in my house, there would be more options to play with, toys to introduce you to, but the greatest toy is the human mind." She was taking to his dominance far better than he could have ever hoped. She pressed into his touch, her thighs parted, breath ragged, her hands curled into fists only to relax again. Needful rocks claimed her hips; her pelvis tipped in before she pushed back with a need to be caressed again.

Michael grabbed a small tube of lube and a fresh condom from his bag and walked back to Lily. Would she be ready for this? This was a simple scene, enough to bring her further into his world, but it was only the beginning. When all of this was over, when the stalker was dealt with, Michael would be able to take her further, deeper into his life and the darkness of his world.

"Need you, Sir," Lily begged.

"Why?" he asked. Would she respond correctly? Would she tell him what was going on? He needed Lily to submit in that way, to communicate and allow him into her mind.

"Hot, so hot inside. Hungry and empty," she responded, her voice a trembling whisper.

It was a start. "It's going to get worse for you before I let you come, Lily. Before I take you." He was watching her as he spoke and smiled. Her thighs tensed, and she bowed her head, hips pressed back as gentle quivers rolled through her body. "You want this."

"Yes, Sir." No hesitation, no hint of denial.

Michael eased onto the bed behind her, his cock eager to plunge into her wet core, his sac tight against the base of his cock. Control. He had to keep control. It would be all too easy to give in and take what he wanted there and then. "Breathe and feel. It's all you have to do. No walls, no holding back."

She murmured something, but he didn't push for her to repeat it. Michael frowned; clear communication was needed at all times, but that was something he could work on over time. Michael settled behind her and ran his hands over her hips before he cupped her buttocks. "Such a sweet sight."

Lily pressed back into his hands, her skin warm and silken beneath his touch. This was a woman he could spend the rest of his life with, if she would only have him. He growled in pleasure as he reached between her thighs and parted her labia. With one finger, he found and circled her clit, teasing her a little at a time before he slid the same finger into her clenching heat. Lily shuddered; her back arched as she moved back against him and rocked onto his finger. She was close, so very close. He could feel it in how she reacted to him, but he wanted to draw the pleasure out.

Michael eased his finger free from her core and opened the condom packet. He smoothed the condom onto his erection and made sure the lube was within reach. "You will not come without permission."

Shadows of the Past

"I understand, Sir." It was a plea more than anything else.

He slipped the tip of his covered cock between her swollen folds and sighed in relief. It didn't matter that he'd already come once. He wanted to, needed to come again. This time with the feel of her walls moving hungrily around his body. Inch by inch he moved into her, waiting every time he felt her respond around him, the tightening enough to drive him insane as he shuddered and focused on his breathing. Only when he was buried to the hilt did he stop and catch his breath. "You've no idea how good it feels to be inside you."

She clenched, her tight walls rippled on his cock, and he almost gave in to his desires.

"Naughty, trying to push me to take you." He slapped one hand down against her still red ass. Her inner walls rippled again. Michael growled, enjoying the feel of her reaction. He struck again and again, adding to the heat that radiated across her buttocks, but it was Lily's reaction he enjoyed the most. Each new spank tightened her sex and tormented him in return. By the time he stopped, his breathing burned in his chest, and his balls were so tight he thought he might explode. Michael forced himself to take a calming breath before he continued. Only when he was ready did he touch the tight rosebud of her ass. "I've taken you everywhere but here, Lily."

Lily whimpered and shook her head.

"You've never had anal sex before, have you?"

"No, Sir. It scares me."

An anal virgin? What else had his Lily not experienced? The idea thrilled him. This was a woman he could teach and mold, but even if she had been more experienced, she would have still been the one for him. "I will be gentle. I won't hurt you. Not like that." There would be some discomfort, but he would build her up slowly until she begged for more. He opened the lube and coated his finger, his cock still buried within her body. Only when he had plenty of lube did he press the tip of his finger against her anus.

"Sir..." she pleaded.

"It's all right. Relax for me; it's all going to work out." He rocked into her body, his finger still pressed against her entrance, though he didn't push in. Instead, he built her heat and his with long, slow strokes in and out of her core. Only when he could feel her body relax did he press the tip of his finger into her back passage.

She jerked, and her head came up as her back and thighs tensed.

"It doesn't hurt, does it, Lily?' He knew it couldn't, not with how little he'd entered her—barely more than the tip—and the amount of lube he'd used would have prevented any pain. "Relax and let me do this."

Slowly she relaxed, obeying him, and her hips began to roll. She rocked back and forth against him, taking his cock with each move and with it his fingertip. He didn't stop her, didn't say anything as he felt her tight, wet sex ripple around his erection. Instead, he let it happen, allowing Lily to build herself back up, to regain her confidence again. Each time she rocked, more of his finger slid into her body, and she groaned.

"The pleasure is building, isn't it? All those nerve endings, the sensations, it's pushing you further each time." Michael wasn't sure how much he could take, but he'd at least introduced her to the start of anal sex. Baby steps. He could handle baby steps right now, at least when it came to pushing her knowledge and experience. "Don't tighten on my finger. You can do it." Her muscles relaxed a bit more, and the tight ring gave under the persistent pressure, allowing his finger to slide home.

Her inner walls clenched, rippled, and a fresh wave of silken heat warmed his cock. "I can't hold back, Sir. I can't."

He slid his finger out of her back passage and grabbed her hips. "Come for me; show me how much you love this. I need to know this is what you want. What you need."

She reacted instantly and bucked beneath him. He held Lily in place, thrusting into her as his balls slapped against her slick, swollen sex. He was home; his Lily had welcomed him home, and he had no intention of ever turning away from her. He growled and claimed her with each new rock of his hips. Her body was his, she

Shadows of the Past

was his, and the pleasure grew until the pressure was more than he could take. Even as his own release threatened, she shuddered beneath him, a small cry torn into life.

It was all he needed.

Michael roared and thrust into Lily's hot, wet sex one last time before his orgasm took control, and he claimed his Lily in all ways that mattered at that moment.

* * * *

Warmth surrounded her, as did Michael's strong arm, and Lily sighed in contentment. The night they had spent together had been far more than she had expected, but now, as she lay in bed knowing she should be awake and moving, she went over the events of the previous night. Michael had taken care of her. Once they had finished, he had released her from the belts and helped her into the shower. There'd been nothing sexual during the shower. He'd washed her down, dried her off, and brought her back to the bed, where he'd held her through the night, there in case she needed him.

Lily didn't open her eyes as she lay on the bed in the safety of his arms. She didn't need to open them to know she was safe in her own bed with a man she had never imagined would be a part of her life. Whatever they had shared was only the beginning. She understood now, knew she couldn't walk away from him, but could she be everything he needed? All he wanted in his life?

I can try.

He hadn't pushed her, hadn't taken her past her comfort zone enough that she would have had to use the traffic light warning system. Yes, he'd prepped her ass, but even then, Michael's desires hadn't been sufficient to push her into saying red or even yellow.

There was no denying how she'd reacted. How her body had submitted to him was something she couldn't explain. Nor did she really have to. Her body and heart knew what she wanted, what she needed, even if a small part of her mind refused to accept what had happened. What if she had turned to Michael only because of the stalker? If what she felt for him wasn't real?

No, she needed Michael in her life, not short term, not for a couple of weeks, but for as long as he'd have her.

Michael's large hand moved and cupped her breast. "You're letting your thoughts take control of you, Lily."

"There's a lot to think through." She didn't pull away from his touch. No, that was the opposite of what she wanted with Michael. His touch triggered a reaction she didn't try to deny. Her nipples hardened, and heat simmered between her thighs, but it wasn't to the point where she'd want to turn and beg for his touch. Not yet at least.

"I can understand." He thumbed her nipple, then moved his hand down to settle it on her waist. "And I won't put any pressure on you."

Pressure to do what? Repeat the experience? "What we did was wonderful, Michael. I've never felt so whole or at peace as I do now." She nestled in against him and sighed. "This is something I didn't even know I was searching for." She had to find the right words because the last thing she wanted was Michael to misunderstand what she was trying to say.

"That's good to hear." His grip tightened, then relaxed. "I don't want to ever let you go, but I know I'll have to."

She twisted in his arms. She had to look at him, to put the pieces together, so she knew what was going on. "Why?'

"Because the job will come to an end, and I'll have to return home. My job means I must be able to report to the office when I'm not away on an assignment. God, the idea of leaving you behind kills me." His voice trembled, and he couldn't meet her gaze. "I knew how dangerous it was to become involved with you, but I walked into this choice with my eyes wide open."

What was he talking about? She touched the side of his face, cupping his cheek. "Who says we have to part when this job is over? I certainly don't want it to end, and I'd never ask you to leave your job."

Shadows of the Past

"And I wouldn't ask you to give up your work, Lily. I know how important it is to you, and an artist without her art dies inside. A vital part of you would cease to exist, and I couldn't ever ask you to do that." He finally met her gaze. "It has to end. Neither of us would be happy with a part-time, meet-up-occasionally type of relationship. There would be too many questions, problems that would build up, and they would eventually destroy us."

A manic giggle threatened to spill into life. He didn't understand how she worked, had no grasp of the situation, which didn't make sense for such an intelligent man. "Michael—"

"No, let me speak. What we have together is all we're ever going to have, but it doesn't mean I'm happy with having to walk away." His eyes glistened.

"Michael, you need to listen to me." She pressed one finger against his lips. "You're making assumptions here based on limited and incorrect information."

He frowned, the lines furrowing between his brows.

"Yes, you can't move, but I can, and I can do it without upsetting my work. I'm a freelancer, Michael. I don't need to be here to work with my clients; it's something I can do anywhere in the world, as long as I have access to high-speed Internet and services like UPS or FedEx. Sure, I go to a few events, not as many as it seems because this month has been busy. I can set up an event like a sip-and-paint just about anywhere in the country if there isn't one already running, and the one we did the other day was a one-off, to begin with. A test to see if it was going to work."

"Wait a minute, what are you saying? You'd move in with me?"

She swallowed down the moment of fear. "I'd move to be with you, not immediately in, but to the same town. A short-term lease, because I don't want to crowd you. I'd need to find a place that would work for both of us in case your home, apartment, or wherever you live, doesn't work for two people when one of them needs a particular type of space to work in." She brushed her fingers over his cheek. Was she doing the right thing? Could she spend the rest of her life with this man?

I don't want to lose him.

But was she ready to move in with him?

It's why I'm giving us both time. Better to have my own place to begin with and take it from there.

She could live with that and hoped he could as well.

"God, are you sure this is what you want?" Michael leaned in to her touch, his voice tender, eyes gentle. "I love you, Lily, but I don't want you to feel like this is something you have to do."

"Yes. I love you, and I've never been so sure of anything in all my life."

Shadows of the Past

Chapter Thirteen

Four days. Four amazing days Michael could never have hoped for, and yet they had been all he had ever wanted and more. With the convention a couple of weeks away and the backed-up commissions, Lily had spent her days working, but the nights... Ah, the nights had been theirs. She'd given him all she could, allowed him to push a little more. Though he hadn't taken their play as far as he'd wanted with the lack of toys and space, she had embraced everything he had shown her.

They'd talked about everything, from music to books, fantasies to pipe dreams, and a thousand things in between. There'd been a few things they hadn't shared an interest in, but they were minor, and no couple was identical when it came to likes and dislikes. Now all they had to do was decide where they wanted to live, or rather where Lily wanted to live. They'd spent some time exploring options online, but it would take a visit or three before Lily would find a place. She'd also made it clear she wouldn't sell her house to begin with, a decision he agreed with one hundred percent. Better to for Lily to feel safe with the ability to return to a place she called her own if things broke down between them.

Michael would do everything he could to prevent it from happening, but he was a realist. Shit happened. That was life, and he wasn't foolish enough, even in love, to believe he could keep them together if they weren't meant to be.

And they were in love. They'd admitted it and embraced it. Michael had never believed he would find the time when he could say that, not after what had happened, but he no longer thought about Ophelia except when he forced himself to. Nor did her loss hurt anymore. It wasn't that he didn't regret her death, but long talks with Lily had taught him he shouldn't blame himself. It hadn't been his fault, but Ophelia's choice and nothing else.

"So, when do I get to meet this Mags?" Lily walked out of her studio and into the kitchen.

"She's going to come down a couple of days before the convention, maybe toward the end of next week." Michael turned and smiled, his body hungering at the sight of the woman he had claimed as his own. "Thank you for accepting the fact we'd need help at the con. It's a weight off my mind." The event would still be hard work, but at least he'd have someone on his side he could trust and would fit in with the geek crowd.

"Mags sounds like an interesting woman." Lily moved through the kitchen and cleared away a few things. "We'll have to leave soon if I'm going to make the meeting on time."

A meeting he wasn't happy about, especially as Lily didn't want him in the room with her. "Yeah, I know."

"Don't be mad, please. I know the office and staff at the agency very well, and I won't be alone. You can watch me walk into the building, then you'll be there when I come out again." She moved behind him and wrapped her arms around his waist. "I've been in and out of the office more times than I care to remember, and this meeting needs to be in person. There are things I want cleared up, and I need to sever the working relationship with Daniel once and for all. It means not working with John either, but if the man has any sense, he'll get out of Daniel's agency ASAP. If you're there, the tensions will rack up higher and faster than I can control. I don't need that, and the rest of the staff there doesn't deserve it."

"Yeah, I understand and agree, but I still don't like it." Sure, she was right. Daniel couldn't stand Michael and already blamed him for what had gone wrong between himself and Lily. If Michael was there, then there would be an argument, and even if he didn't say a word, it would blow up. Not something he wanted, but the idea of her being in the building without him knotted his stomach.

"You don't have to like it, Michael." Lily nestled her head against his back. "We'll get through this and be stronger for it. Maybe when I can get out of the office, we can go somewhere for dinner?"

Michael rested one hand on top of hers. "Sure, it sounds like a good idea." As long as they came back here after the meal, then he could spend the rest of the night showing Lily just how deeply he loved her.

An hour later, Michael pulled up outside of the office building and parked in the small lot. Lily had been calm during the drive through town, and he had been careful not to do anything that might turn her sense of peace into nerves or worse. "You ready for this?"

"No, but it needs to be done. Daniel has been a huge part of my life, but it's time to sever our arrangement once and for all. Maybe by doing such, he can find a sense of himself again and focus on his new clients. Ones he doesn't have a personal relationship with." Lily sighed and unbuckled her seatbelt. "I think it's where the problem started. We were friends first and foremost, and it got in the way of business. Maybe he believed he was actually trying to help me, that this was for the best. But he forgot everything he knew about me, all the things we'd been through, and he forgot to come to me and ask what I actually wanted."

Michael nodded. Maybe she was right, but his gut said something else: Daniel had other ideas about their relationship. "Well, I'll be right here when you've finished."

"I know, and I'm grateful." Lily twisted in her seat and reached for him; one hand slid into his hair, her grip firm as she used it to pull him close. The Dominant in him debated resisting, saying it was wrong to allow a submissive to take control, but with a silent *screw you* to that voice, he accepted her insistent tug and let her claim his lips. She whimpered against him. Her back arched before she pulled back and released her grip. "Sorry, I needed something to see me through this mess."

"Nothing to be sorry for." He met her gaze and smiled. "You can do this."

Lily took a deep breath and exited the car. She paused at the door to the office building, turned, and waved before she vanished inside.

Michael sighed and settled back in the driver's seat. His skin tightened and itched as he waited. There was nothing wrong here. Lily had been to the office time and again. She knew people here, and it was a public location. What could go wrong?

Anything and everything.

He watched the door but let his gaze move over the windows, checking them for signs of trouble. Lily had shared with him the lay-out of the office as she knew it, though obviously, she hadn't been to every room in the structure. The area that was rented by Daniel and his team took over five offices on the left-hand side of the second floor. Three other businesses shared the location, spread over the two floors, and a search on them showed nothing that raised any alarms. Yet he still couldn't throw off the discomfort as it built between his shoulder blades.

Overprotective Dom. That's what this is. She's strong; she must be able to handle this on her own. I can't walk in and take it from her. If he tried to join Lily without her asking for his help, it would backfire on him, and she wouldn't forgive him.

Michael tried to relax, but he couldn't turn away from the door. Mentally he kept track of time as he waited, refusing to put the radio on or even look at his phone unless it beeped an alert.

Gunshots rang out, cutting through the background noise of the city, and Michael was out of the car. He broke into a run as he made his way to the front door. One hand on the butt of his gun, and it was drawn before he knew what was happening.

Men and women poured out through the door, a trickle at first, then it turned into a rush as the second round of shots split the air.

Second floor.

Lily.

Stop, calm down, assess.

His heart pounded, and he paused long enough to think before he reacted. He didn't know what he was going up against, how many shooters, and he grabbed one of the men as they ran out.

"What happened?"

Shadows of the Past

"Shots. Walker Agency," the middle-aged man gasped, his face white, eyes wide. "Heard a scream. Don't know anything else."

Michael nodded and let go of the man. "Thank you. Get to cover. Call the cops." Someone had likely already made the call, but better to give the order and cover his bases.

The man fled without another word.

Lily.

He had to get in there and find out what had happened to Lily.

* * * *

"Daniel," Lily said in the way of a greeting as she settled into a chair opposite the man she had once counted as a friend.

"Lily, I'm glad you could make it. We need to talk." Daniel smiled, though it didn't reach his eyes. "Things haven't been good between us, not in the last week or so, and I need to— No, I want to make it right. We've been through too much, and I don't want to throw this away."

Is that what he believed? He wanted to make it right? "Daniel, don't get me wrong. We've been friends for a long time, but you've done some things that don't sit right with me." She kept her voice calm as she watched her one-time friend. "All those contracts signed without my consent? I know you meant well, but it wasn't part of the agreement, and you all but worked me into the ground."

"Now you're overreacting, girl. I took care of you, dealt with the side of the business you didn't want to handle. You can't cope with the paperwork and deal with the creative side. It's not in your nature."

Girl? Even at this moment when he knew things were bad between them, he referred to her as if she were a child. Her hands clenched in her lap, and she forced herself to take a deep breath. "Daniel, I've asked you a hundred times and more not to call me girl."

The door opened behind her as she watched Daniel's jaw tighten. "It's a habit, Lily. Besides, you *are* a girl."

"No, I'm a woman, and there's a huge difference. How would

you like it if I called you boy?"

"That's not the same thing," Daniel blustered and stared at the door. "Ah, John, glad you could make it. Sit down, please. Hopefully, we can get this over and done with." He gestured to the other chair.

"Yes, it is the same thing. Girl, boy, they're both terms for children. If I called you boy, you'd be upset, but you think nothing of calling me a girl, and you started doing it a lot in the last two years." Would the man never learn?

"So, you want to break up a strong working relationship because I slip now and then and call you a girl?" Daniel shook his head in disbelief.

"I don't think that's what she's saying, Daniel," John suggested as he slipped into the chair. "At least, it's not what I'm hearing."

Daniel scowled, a dismissive noise erupting from his throat. "Of course that's not what you're hearing. You're looking forward to working with Lily instead of me."

Lily glanced down at her hands, still clenched, in her lap. Daniel wasn't being reasonable. "I won't be working with John either. I think a clean break from the agency is for the best."

John whistled through clenched teeth before he spoke. "Are you sure it's a good idea? I mean, you've been with us for years, Lily. Moving to another agency or manager is going to cause a lot of upset."

"And leaving my work here will cause more. Daniel is personally involved in all of this. I don't think having Daniel continue to deal with me as a client, but my files being handled by someone else, would help this entire situation." She forced her voice to remain calm. This wasn't easy, but Lily had known it wouldn't be from the moment she'd made her decision. "I've looked at this from every angle I can think of. Daniel won't be happy with me working with you, John. Which will increase tensions in the office." She turned enough to catch John's gaze. "I don't want to do that to you or anyone else."

"This is Michael's doing, isn't it?" Daniel asked from between clenched teeth. John shifted in his chair beside Lily.

"No, it has nothing to do with—"

"Don't lie to me, Lily. Not after all we've been through together." Daniel cut her off.

"I'm not lying. We've been having problems for the last year at least." Lily gestured from herself to Daniel. What was wrong with the man?

"No, it's this Michael. I've heard the reports, seen it with my own eyes, and there's no denying it. When that man walked into your life, you changed. Are you sleeping with him? Is that the hold he has over you? Well, it won't last. I've reported him to the company he works for. I'm confident he will lose his job soon enough. I doubt they allow their people to fuck their clients. Not exactly professional, is it?"

Reports? Reports from who, where? Questions burned through her mind as her chest tightened. Had Daniel been spying on her? "I don't understand. Have you—" She coughed and cleared her throat. "Are you the stalker, Daniel? Who has been reporting things to you?" And how much did he know? Was the thing about sex guesswork or something else?

"I've been with you for years, not just as a manager but as a friend. I know more about you than you could ever believe. There isn't a part of your house I'm not familiar with." Daniel rose and planted his hands on the desk. "And if you think I'm going to let you walk away from me after all of this, then you're out of your mind."

"Daniel, calm down. You're being irrational." Her gut rolled. Daniel was the stalker. Why hadn't she seen it before now? He wanted full control over her life. She went back over when the stalker had first appeared. There'd been an argument, nothing major, between herself and Daniel a week, maybe two, before the first signs. Had that been the trigger? A way he could prevent her from finding another manager?

"You can't walk away from everything we've built up together," Daniel protested.

That was it. She had to get out of there and talk to Michael. If Daniel was the stalker, Michael would be able to put the pieces together. She swallowed hard and rose. "I need to leave. I'll send in an official letter, but this conversation is getting us nowhere."

"No, Lily, sit, please. I'm sure I can calm Daniel down. Then you and I can figure things out. I don't see a reason why Daniel would need to be involved in things if I take over your workload." John rose and his voice shook. "You don't want to throw it all away."

She didn't glance at him, didn't dare, not with how strange Daniel was acting. "No, I don't think there's any other logical choice. There has to be a clean break, so we can all walk away from this before it gets out of hand." She had to get out of the office before the situation exploded. Lily forced her hands to relax before she met Daniel's gaze. "We've been friends for a long time, and I hope we can rebuild our friendship when all this is over and done with."

"You're hurting yourself, my girl. You'll realize it when he dumps you," Daniel snarled.

Something touched her arm, then tightened into a grip. Lily scowled and turned, uncertain what was happening.

John. Calm, easy to work with John had a painful hold on her arm. "What's going..." Her voice trailed off as she realized what she was seeing.

John had a gun.

"You can't walk away from me, Lily. Not after everything we've built between us."

It didn't make sense. Was he drunk? "John, put the gun down."

"No, you're coming with me." He tugged on her arm and pulled her close.

"John, I don't know what's going on, but Lily's right. You need to put the gun down." Daniel's voice changed from the frantic man about to lose a client to a man who was calm, focused, and determined.

"Shut the fuck up. Thanks to you, I nearly lost her. I'm not going to let that happen." John waved the gun in Daniel's direction.

Shadows of the Past

"Don't try to stop me. I'm done playing your game, and I'm not going to let that thug you brought into her life get anywhere near her again. I know what she needs. What she's always needed."

John? How could John suddenly have flipped? She didn't move, didn't dare, not with the gun John had in his hand. The man wasn't stable right now, though she had no idea what had triggered the change. "John, let me go. Please. Whatever is going on here, this isn't the way to deal with it."

He jerked her back toward the door. "We're leaving. We're going to talk, but it's not going to be here."

No, I can't let him take me out of here. Lily twisted and tried to force him to let go of her, but John tightened his grip on her arm. She winced. "You're hurting me."

"Don't fight me. I don't want to hurt you, Lily. I've never wanted to hurt you, but you'll leave me no choice if you try to get away from me." His voice dropped into a cold whisper.

"John, put the fucking gun down, now!" Daniel moved from behind his desk.

It all happened so fast Lily didn't have a chance to react until it was over. The gun went off, once, twice, and Daniel stumbled back against the wall.

Blood. There was blood, but she didn't have a chance to see clearly as John forced her out toward the door. Screams, yells, and the scrapes of chairs all mingled into one as she stumbled with John, still held in his grasp. A cold sweat coated her flesh as she moved, her heart racing, throat tight. Whatever John had in mind, she had to remain calm. She couldn't try to go for the gun.

Was Daniel dead?

No, she couldn't think about that right now.

A sound caught her attention, forcing Lily to focus on the others in the office.

"John, what's... Oh God." A woman's voice. Two more shots and screams filled the air.

Stay calm, stay alive, and I'll get out of this.

Michael would come for her. She knew it in her gut. He wouldn't let John hurt her. All she had to do was hold on and do what she was told until Michael found her.

* * * *

Michael pulled out his phone and hit Harvey's number. He spoke as soon as he heard the line pick up. "Shots fired. Lily's in Walker's agency. Heading in. Alert the team." He didn't wait for an answer as he ended the call, put the phone on silence, checked the entrance to the building, and walked in, gun at the ready.

Calm. Do this by the numbers.

His mind entered the same hyperalert state he associated both with Dom space and being in the line of fire as he stepped into the main hall. He kept to the walls, his steps cat-footed as he made his way to the stairs. No elevator in the building, which was a plus, but there was more than one entrance and exit.

Shouldn't be doing this on my own. By the numbers would mean waiting for backup.

But there was no one else unless he waited for the cops, and then it would either be too late or they wouldn't let him in.

Not something he was going to risk.

Michael moved slowly through the building as he made his way to the first set of stairs. He kept to the side, taking it one step at a time, his senses at full alert. Each sound, every scent came to him clearly. Soft sobs, the smell of blood and gunshot, urine and fear, all combined into something he'd hoped Lily would never be exposed to.

Was she dead, lying in a pool of her own blood?

No, he wasn't going to think of that. Lily was alive, and he'd find her. She was smart. She must have taken cover when the shooting had begun. Even now she would be waiting for the all clear, and then he'd find her and bring her back down to his car where it was safe. He'd take her home and never let her come to harm again. All he had to do was get her out of here in one piece.

He stepped up onto the next floor. Three doors to the left; one

Shadows of the Past

to the right. The one to the right was the main door in and out of the agency, but to get there, he'd have to make it past one open door on the left. He moved silently to the first door and took the time to clear the room. Empty. Signs of scattered furniture and papers, but whoever had been working in the office had already fled.

Best thing to do in situations like this was to either flatten down and wait it out or get the hell out of Dodge as soon as you could.

His attention turned to the door that led into the office. By rights, he should have cleared the other two rooms, but a low groan of pain drew his attention. It didn't sound like Lily, but someone was in there, someone who might be able to tell him what had happened. Michael moved with care, checking all points as he made his way into the office and through the first room, a reception area from the layout.

"H-help me." A weak voice, male, from the back of the offices.

Michael paused; did he know the voice? He frowned but didn't hurry. There were signs of chaos all around the room as he walked toward the back of the agency.

"Please, someone help me. He's bleeding," a female voice, one he didn't know, called out. "He's been shot. Is there anyone there?"

"I'm coming in. I need you to make sure your hands are where I can see them. I'm armed security." The last thing he would ever do was claim to be a cop, but better the woman and whoever was hurt realized he was on the right side of things, not another source of danger. "Cops are on the way." Or at least they should be.

"Yes, I understand," the woman replied. There was a chance the woman was the shooter, but he doubted it. She was obviously shaken, and more than likely she was a witness caught up in all of this.

Michael moved slowly through the room to the back of the office, checking for signs of the gunman, but all signs suggested the shooter was gone.

Where's Lily?

She wasn't the one shot. At least not the one who had called out. That had been a male voice. Michael's chest tightened. Could she be injured or dead?

A woman, early thirties maybe, knelt by the side of a male figure, her blood-smeared hands lifted into the air. "Here, we're here."

Michael cleared the room and checked both of them. "Okay, get pressure on the wounds." He stared at the man and frowned. Daniel. "What happened? Have you seen Lily?"

"John; it was John. He had a gun. Shot Daniel and took Lily," the woman explained; tears streamed down her face. "I don't know why. It all happened so fast. I think he went for his car. I don't know."

The distant wail of sirens caught Michael's attention, but he didn't turn away from Daniel and the woman. "Sounds like help will be here soon. Stay with Daniel." He turned and left the room, picking up the pace as he headed for the corridor.

John had Lily.

John's the stalker.

It was the only thing that made sense. Michael kicked himself as he moved through the building. He hadn't seen anything in John's behavior that had triggered a warning. John had been attentive, but not in a creepy way. John hadn't even had a problem with Michael being at the coffee-shop event. What the hell had Michael missed with the guy?

And now he had Lily.

* * * *

Lily didn't struggle as John hurried her through the building and out toward the back stairs. She tensed for a moment when she realized the route wouldn't take her out toward the parking lot at the front of the office where Michael would be able to see her. Lily forced herself to relax. Panic or struggles wouldn't help. She had to keep her head if she wanted a chance to live through this.

"We'll talk when we're away from here. Oh, we have so much to talk about, to plan out." John smiled—actually smiled—as they left the building and hurried across the back road to a smaller, gravel-covered lot. He kept the gun pressed to her side as he led her to the cars. "It's all going to work out, you'll see. You'll thank me when we're settled. I know you will."

Lily didn't answer as her mind reeled. He was happy about this, or at least seemed to be now they were away from the office.

"Get in the car and keep your hands where I can see them." He stepped away from Lily enough to allow her to move but kept the gun trained on her. He gestured to the passenger-side door as he reached into his pocket with his free hand to hit the fob on his key ring. "I know you're not happy right now, but you will be when we're away from all of this."

Keep him calm, agree with him, but do it slowly, so he doesn't get suspicious.

He wouldn't kill her, at least not yet, and anything she could do to stay alive long enough for Michael to find her was worth doing. Lily complied with John's instructions and walked to the passenger side of the car, followed by John. He held the gun trained on her as she moved and got into the car. Lily glanced back at John and gave him a nervous smile as she kept her hands in her lap. John pulled something out of his pocket, the keys jangling. Her gaze narrowed on the zip-tie handcuffs, the type she'd seen on various shows, but she didn't move.

"Lift up your hands."

She obeyed and licked her bottom lip nervously. "You don't need to cuff me, John."

"Yes, I do. It's for our safety. I think you know that." John slipped the cuffs around her wrists and closed them. Not enough to cut the blood flow but certainly enough to prevent her from sliding her hands free. "We'll be safe, both of us. All you have to do is listen to me, and we'll be away from all of this soon enough."

"John, I'll go anywhere with you. You know I will." *Keep calm, and Michael will find me.*

"I know you will. You see the sense in all of this." John closed the door and moved around the car to step into the driver's side. A moment later he was behind the wheel, and they were moving. "I need you to stay calm. We don't need to get involved in an accident, do we?"

"No, of course not." She kept her bound hands in her lap. Lily tried to appear calm. John had the gun within easy reach, but at the same time, she kept an eye on the route. John obviously had a plan or at least an idea of where he was going to take her. He hadn't let her grab her small bag, but there would be other ways of getting a message out to Michael. There had to be. She knew his number by heart now, and all she had to do was grab a phone and do something, anything, that would alert the man she loved to where she was.

John didn't say anything for a time as they traveled away from the office, and the first signs of trouble, in the form of sirens, caused the man to curse under his breath, but he didn't do anything that would alert the approaching first responders. Instead, he outwardly remained calm and followed the rules of the road, going above speed limit by one or two miles an hour to not arouse suspicion.

"They won't come after us immediately. I have time. They might not even put out an alert for a while or think I've stayed close to the office, but they don't know me. Don't know you."

Michael knew her though. "Sounds reasonable." Lily kept her tone light and conversational. Where was he going? She glanced at the names of the roads. North. They were heading north, but he would avoid the interstates and main roads. They were more likely to have cameras on them. But John had lived in the area for a long time, so probably knew all the shortcuts, as would his wife—*His wife!*

"John, won't your wife be worried about you when you don't come home?"

John's hand clenched, knuckles white as he continued to steer. "No."

What was her name? Shit, I've only met her a couple of times. Sharon. That was it. Sharon. "But Sharon will worry unless she's away. I wouldn't want her upset with me."

"She won't be." He grunted. "Close your eyes. I want you rested

Shadows of the Past

for tonight. Our first night together."

Chapter Fourteen

Michael waited outside of the office building as the police and EMTs made their way in and out. Every instinct screamed at him to try to follow John, to find him and pull Lily out of the situation, but there was nothing Michael could do until the police released him. Something he hoped would happen sooner rather than later, but he'd already been held for nearly twenty minutes since he'd returned after finding out John's car was gone.

He'd been too late.

Lily. Hold on. Wherever you are, please hold on. I'll find you.

He had to find her. Life without her didn't bear thinking about.

His jacket pocket vibrated, and he frowned before he pulled the phone out. A quick glance at the screen told him it was Harvey. "Boss?"

"Mags is on the way in. She's maybe five minutes out."

Michael frowned at the phone. "What? How's that possible?"

"She was already in town, visiting friends, but she's heading over now." The calm voice of the older man carried through the phone. "Don't leave until she's there. I don't want you trying to do this on your own. Better to have someone with you who can back you up and someone you trust."

Mags was both of those. Like all the men and women who worked for Harvey, Mags was highly trained, calm, and competent. Michael had worked with her at least a dozen times in the last year alone. "Got it. I'll wait for her." If nothing else, Mags would help to keep him on track, and he wasn't foolish enough to think he wouldn't need backup.

"You better. I know you care for Ms. Elliot and—"

"I love her, Harvey. I love Lily."

Silence claimed the line except for a few crackles until Harvey coughed. "I thought it was something like that. John Wash and Daniel Walker both sent in reports suggesting you were being inappropriate with Ms. Elliot. I assured them if there was a problem, Ms. Elliot would say such, and I would reach out to her in the coming week to make sure all was well. Neither of them took kindly to that."

No, Michael didn't imagine they had. "Understood." Shit, this wasn't the time or place, but he had to get this out in the open. "I didn't force her, and God alone knows I tried to keep my distance, Harvey. But fuck. What's between us is more than I could ignore. More than either of us could ignore." He rubbed the back of his neck and scanned the crowd, moving from cop to cop, taking in the EMTs and the view he still had of Daniel in the back of the ambulance.

"I get it, believe me. If you are meant to be, then I won't stand in your way. Not now, not ever. But right now, I need your head in the game. If your Lily is to come home safe to you, you have to treat this as if the kidnap victim is someone you have little or no emotional connection to," Harvey said.

Bullshit. Oh, how Michael wanted to snap at his boss, but at the same time, a part of him agreed with the older man. "I'll do my best, chief."

"I mean it, Michael. Use your head, not your heart."

Michael took a deep breath and nodded. "Got it. I'm not going to let anything happen to her."

"Mr. Parker?" Detective Richmond made his way through the crowd.

"Gotta go. Local cops want to talk to me." Michael ended the call, pocketed the phone, and waited for the detective to reach him. "Yes?"

"You're cleared to leave."

"Not happening until I know more." Michael's jaw tightened.

"You need to stay out of this," the middle-aged man insisted.

Michael's hands clenched into fists, and he forced them to return to a more normal position. "Would you stay out of it if the victim was the woman you loved?" There, it was public. "Besides the fact I'm supposed to be protecting her. The man who took her may be tied into this situation in other ways."

"The stalker, you mean? Yeah, it crossed my mind." Richmond sighed and gestured for Michael to follow him away from prying eyes. "Look, this goes against procedure, but yeah, we're pretty sure he's the stalker—at least from what they've been able to find at his house so far. Daniel also confirmed that John's wife left him about a year ago. John's entire focus became work and his clients."

"Any sign of Lily at John's house?"

"Nothing to suggest she's ever been there, but there are plenty of photographs, pieces of artwork, stolen clothing, and a lot more. It all suggests he's fixated on Ms. Elliot and has been for a long time."

Michael knew well enough that stalkers didn't need a reason. They made the connections themselves. A smile at the wrong moment, a glance, a touch, it all added up to something far more in the mind of a man like John. "Any criminal record?"

"No, and we're checking for anything registered in his name, property wise, other than the house. There's also a BOLO for the car with an observe but do not approach."

Why was the detective telling him this? Michael had an idea but wanted to hear it from Richmond's lips. "You're bringing me in. Why?"

"Because time is of the essence right now, and your people, your firm, might have resources we can't tap." Richmond met Michael's gaze, his jaw set. "And we're going to need all the help we can get."

Michael nodded as the rest went unsaid, but he knew what Richmond was talking about. "Got it. A colleague of mine is on her way and..." He paused as he spotted a car pulling up, one he recognized. "I think she's here."

"Good, you shouldn't be dealing with this alone. Not with the emotions involved."

"No arguments there."

* * * *

Shadows of the Past

John continued to talk about how things would be better once they arrived. His tension eased as the route took them out of town and toward the country. He avoided the major roads, which reduced the chances of them being spotted by traffic cameras once they were beyond the more heavily traveled areas. Not something that sat well with Lily, but there was nothing she could do. The doors were locked, and her hands were secured. She didn't have a weapon, cell phone, or anything else she could use.

Except for her mind.

The roads changed as they continued, turning into narrower country roads, then to dirt roads. Lily shifted carefully in her seat and tried to take note of where they were.

Farmland.

Where the hell was he taking her?

"Wait until you see what I have set up for us. I know it's a place you'll like, and then you can relax. I have a room arranged for you, for your art. No computers, of course, but I think you'll be more at peace when you return to traditional art. You've needed this, a means of getting away from it all. The pressure will be gone, lifted from your shoulders. I've wanted to do it for a long time, save you from the stress, I mean, but when she left, I realized what I was supposed to do."

"You mean Sharon?" Lily had to understand; it was the only chance she had to get into his mind.

"Yes, Sharon. Bitch. I gave her everything she could ever want. She didn't have to do a thing unless she wanted to, but it was never enough. It would never be enough. Said I was smothering her, crushing the life out of her by not letting her do things for herself." John snorted and made a sharp turn onto a road that was barely more than a track. "I tried. I really tried, but she threw it all in my face. Then she leaves, just leaves without giving me a chance to find out what I could do to make her happy."

Oh God, he's done something like this before with his wife.

How had the people John worked with not known what was happening? Had Sharon reported the situation? But then again what would there be to report? Sure, it was a form of abuse. Anyone with a brain could understand that, but it wasn't the type that—as far as she knew—the police could do anything about. Would it come under emotional abuse? It would make sense, and a divorce lawyer might have been able to deal with that as a means of filing for divorce, but not the police.

"She was wrong, wasn't she? I need you to tell me she was wrong to walk out on me." John's voice bordered on frantic.

"Yes, of course she was," Lily agreed quickly. John was insane, but he'd hidden it for a long time.

"Good, see, you can see it. I know it makes no sense for Sharon to leave. No, there had to be someone else who had come into her life, like that Michael of yours. Yes, that's what happened. I know it in my heart. She would never have left otherwise."

Michael. How is he going to find me? Lily tried to think straight, to keep herself calm as they drove down the driveway that led through what appeared to be an abandoned farmstead.

"Michael. He's wrong for you. I've seen how he is. What he does to people," John continued on as he pulled to a stop in front of an old two-story farmhouse. "But you're going to be safe here, away from him and others like him." He unlocked the car. "I'll take the cuffs off you when I know you're going to stay calm."

Lily swallowed down her fear. She had to play along, if only for a time. "Yes, I understand why you're doing this, John. This is all for my own safety." Lily waited until he came around to her side of the car and got out when he opened the door. Every inch of her screamed she should run, escape, take the risk and break free, but he had a gun, and she couldn't outrun a bullet. "I'll do what you want."

"I knew you were the right one. I knew it from the start, but I tried to be a decent husband to Sharon and not look at other women." John took hold of her arm and led the way to the door. "But you'll like this. I've set it all up for you, and I know you're going to be happy with me. We're both going to be so very happy."

* * * *

"I've got it," Mags informed Michael from the passenger seat. "North of the city looks like twenty miles outside. Rural area." Her gaze was fixed on the screen. "Take the…" She rattled off instructions before she glanced over at Michael. "Need that repeated?"

"No." The single word was clipped. Hacking into the system, which allowed them to track the built-in phone system that was a part of the vehicle John was using, fell into those resources Detective Richmond had mentioned. Sure, the police might be able to do the same thing, but only after getting a judge to sign off on it. Then they'd still have to wait until the company checked with legal, made sure their asses were covered, and all of that took time.

Something they could ill afford.

"She's going to get through this," Mags said.

"I know. There's no other option." He glanced at the woman. Mags's shoulder-length blue-black hair had been pulled back into a small ponytail to keep it back from her olive-touched skin and deep brown eyes. "I'm going to get her back, no matter the cost."

"I know, but you still need to think with your head, not your heart, Michael. Shit, I know it's dangerous. God alone knows I've made more than a few dumbass mistakes because of love in the past, but this is where we could both end up dead and your woman with us." Her voice was cold, calmer than he had ever heard it before, which was a warning he understood all too clearly.

"Lily is my heart."

Mags shifted in her seat. "Yes, I know. Anyone with half a brain could see that, but she isn't going to want you to get yourself killed."

"Not going to happen." No, he needed to get Lily to safety; then there'd be time they could both relax. Whatever the cost, he'd pay it. Him. No one else. Not Lily and not Mags. "My head's in the right place, Mags."

"It better be, or I'm going to kick your ass from here to the other side of the state and back again."

He had no doubt she'd try. Mags was one of the most determined women he'd ever met, and she went head to head with the rest of Harvey's people whenever she had to. "Yeah, I know you will."

"I think he's stopped at a possible farmhouse," she informed him as they drew closer. "Maybe a farmstead? One that's been left behind after the rest of the land has been sold off? I can't see this being an actual, fully working farm. There'd be too many people around, if that were the case."

With so many smaller farms being bought out over the years, there were often separate farmsteads left behind. Some went to rot and ruin, but others either remained with the original family or were sold off. "If it's an older place with good windbreaks, we'll be approaching with heavy tree coverage around the main building." A natural windbreak was standard in this area—older trees that had been left to grow close to the house. They were twenty to forty feet away from the actual buildings but still close enough to help shelter the house and any other structures from the blasts of the winter winds.

"That will help and hinder us at the same time. We won't know if there are any traps John might have set up, but we also know he's going to be on his own." Mags glanced up from the screen.

"Do we?" God, what if they were wrong?

"He's a stalker, and from what we've been able to find out so far, he's a loner. It's exceedingly rare for stalkers to work with anyone else. It's not in their nature, but it doesn't mean we shouldn't be on the lookout for trouble," Mags explained, her voice still calm. "We're not stupid, Michael. We're professionals, and we'll handle this like any other job. That means using everything we've learned over the years. Not just on our own but from everyone else. All the tricks we've had drummed into us."

"Preaching to the choir, Mags."

"Yeah, right." She tapped the screen. "Got it. We're looking for a turning on the left, little more than a track, according to the map.

Shadows of the Past

Three buildings. One house, one barn, and maybe a wellhouse. It's small, whatever it is."

It was all he needed to know.

* * * *

Lily's jaw dropped, though she got herself under control quickly as John led her into the house. From the outside, the farmhouse had appeared rundown with a few newer repairs, but inside was a different matter. New carpet, the furniture seemed to be clean and fresh, curtains, signs of life and care. Not what she'd expected, but John made it clear he'd been preparing the place for a while.

"It's beautiful, isn't it? I told you I'd prepared things for you." John let go of her arm and closed the door behind them. "I've been here at least two days a week. Wait until you see the studio. I've got it all set up the way you like it."

"This is wonderful, thank you." *Stay happy, calm, let him think I want to be here.* How long had John been working on this? It wasn't cheap to buy all of this or do any repairs on the house. Come to think of it, who owned the place? Was it John's, or did it belong to someone else? No, it had to be his. If he were renting, there was always a chance the landlord would stumble on what was going on here. Not a risk John would take. "Is this your place?"

"Yes, yes. Oh, you wouldn't believe how Sharon hated this place. She said that was the final straw. Claimed I would keep her here, wouldn't allow her to leave. She didn't understand I was try-ing to protect her. There's so much danger out there. You've seen it. You saw how that man treated you, how he used you for sex."

Heat flushed across her cheeks. Michael hadn't used her, would never use her, but John didn't want to hear that. "We all make mis-takes." A soft tremble ran through her body as she stood, her wrists still restrained by the zip-tie cuffs.

"Yes, we all do. Sharon was mine, but I've paid for it. I cleansed myself, and Michael was yours. I can help cleanse you, relieve you of his taint. I know you need it too; your skin crawls from his touch. He pushed you into places you didn't want to go. I know that about you. I know how dangerous it is to allow the wrong person into your life."

Life, not heart. Of course, he believed she'd been forced. "I need time. That's all, John. Peace and quiet."

"I can do more than give you time, Lily." He returned to her side and cupped her face. "Let me clean you of his touch. I can make it all go away if you let me."

Fear wrapped itself around her heart. What was he doing? She tensed, hands clenched into fists as she struggled not to react to him.

"Do you want to be cleansed, Lily? I know you do." He moved closer, his face almost touching hers. "All you have to do is relax and let it happen." His lips claimed hers.

Lily pulled away, shaking her head. "No. Please no. I'm not ready for this."

"Slut," John snarled and shoved Lily away. "Little whore. You gave yourself to him."

Lily hit the floor hard, her head connecting with the wood. Stars danced in front of her eyes, and she lay there, unable to move.

"You stupid little bitch!" John stalked toward her, eyes dark, jaw clenched.

"No, it's not like that, John. I need a couple of days to adjust. I'm— I'm not worthy of your kiss right now."

He blinked, and his entire demeanor changed. John softened as he watched her. "Oh, yes, of course, I understand now." John reached down and grabbed her by the wrists before he pulled Lily back to her feet. "It's all right, my love. I understand. I truly understand." He pulled her in against his chest and cradled her, one hand cupped against the back of her head. "It's all going to be all right. All you have to do is listen to me, obey me, and love me. It's all I've ever wanted, Lily. Your love. You know it, don't you? I know you do."

Lily wanted to protest, to say that she would never come to love John. She loved Michael, not the asshole who had grabbed her at gunpoint. But she had to wait, find a way to survive until Michael

Shadows of the Past

found her.

No matter what it took.

* * * *

"We've tracked John's car to a farmhouse outside town." Michael rattled off the address as Richmond listened on the other end of the phone. "He's in there. We think he's on his own."

"You think?" Richmond's voice was cold and professional.

"No signs of anyone else, only the one car, and I don't think he'd trust anyone else with Lily." *Please, let me be right about that.*

Mags inclined her head in agreement.

"Yeah, you're probably right. I'm sending out backup, but you're on your own until then." Richmond paused, his voice thicker. "Don't do anything stupid out there and listen out for the cars. We'll run lights and sirens off."

"Understood. We're heading in." Michael ended the call and met Mags gaze. "You ready for this?"

A cold, dangerous smile claimed her lips. "Yes."

"Let's do it."

They moved as one. Each step was taken with care as they moved through the thick line of trees that created a windbreak. The stand was made up of old and new trees, but mostly old. It hadn't been cut back or tended in some time, which made moving in silence difficult. Still, they managed it. All the years of training they had been through, the times they had worked together before this, all added up in a way that allowed them to make it through to the edge.

Mags signaled, and they both paused, half hidden behind trees and undergrowth. Ahead of them lay an empty section of grass with no cover. They'd be out in the open, but the side of the house they approached had no windows on the ground floor. Where there had been one, it was now covered over by planks of wood that blocked the window off with little more than the occasional slit.

A slit someone might be able to watch through.

Had John set up cameras?

God, Michael hoped not. The snatch. Had it been planned or a spur of the moment thing? His instinct said a mixture of both. The kidnapping had been planned, the timing hadn't. With everything else the man had managed, the grab was too disorganized. Too many factors that could have gone wrong. No, Michael's gut said taking Lily at the office had been an impulse, and once John had committed to it, there'd been no going back.

Mags met and held Michael's gaze before she indicated they should split up and approach from either side of the covered window. In silence, they parted and waited for a moment once they were in position before Michael lifted his hand, put up three fingers, and counted down. They moved at the same time, keeping low to the ground as they approached the house, Glocks palmed and steps silent until they flattened themselves against the side of the farmhouse.

Michael edged closer to the covered window and listened, his gaze narrowed. What if John was expecting them? Michael wasn't going to let Lily down. His heart raced even as he tried to push his doubts to the back of his mind. He could do this. Michael wasn't on his own. He had Mags; they'd worked together before, and he trusted his colleague.

Voices, one male, one female, but he couldn't make out the words. He gestured to Mags and indicated two people in the house.

Was there anyone else?

He continued to listen, but no one else joined in the conversation on the other side of the wall. Michael confirmed with Mags that he was still hearing only two people, and they moved around the house. There would be doors, at least two, in and out of the building. All they had to do was get in, grab Lily, and get out.

Easy, sure, and I have the winning lottery numbers in my back pocket.

* * * *

"Come with me. Come on. I have something special to show you. I've been working on this for the last five months." John pulled her through the living room toward a door. He paused and flashed a smile. "You're going to like this. I know you are. This is everything you could want. I took careful note, even used my cameras to make sure I hadn't missed anything."

"Cameras?" Lily's heart sank.

"Yes, I put them in so I knew you'd be safe. I've been watching you for a long time. It was the only way I could protect you when I wasn't there." John canted his head and rested one hand against the door. "Are you ready for this?"

Lily nodded, her throat tight. What the hell had he seen with those cameras? Shit. That was how John had known Michael was her lover. He hadn't been guessing. He'd known. He'd seen the way they'd acted together. How she'd responded to Michael's touches, the bond between them, especially in the last few days.

God, John had seen it all.

Were there cameras in her bedroom?

Her stomach rolled at the thought. If that were true, the cops would be able to see it all. They'd go through the files, if they found them, and then they would all know what she had done with Michael. Cold shivers ran through her body as she tried to come to terms with the things she had learned. If there were recordings of herself and Michael out there, she'd deal with it. No, they'd deal with it. Michael wouldn't let her go through this alone.

John pushed the door open and led Lily into the room.

Her heart skipped a beat and, despite the circumstances, the artist in her squealed in joy, though no sound slipped from her lips. It was all there except a computer. A large glass art table with an adjustable angle, a light box, pens and pencils ranging from student quality to high-end brands she had used in her work. Paper ranged from cold-press watercolor to sketching paper of various types. Charcoals, paints, and brushes all lined the shelves, laid out so they could be easily seen. She swallowed hard. This wasn't cheap, not by any stretch of the imagination. There were easily tens of thousands of dollars' worth of equipment and supplies in the room, if not more. She wouldn't know until she explored in depth.

God, the markers alone would have set John back two thousand with the range of colors and inking pens.

"Do you like it?" John stepped farther into the room and turned to look at her. "I think I have everything you need here, and if I don't, I'll order it for you. Anything you want will be yours."

Except a computer and the means to escape.

"Lily?"

"It's...wonderful." Had Michael presented this to her, Lily would have been thrilled. But John wasn't the one she was meant to be with. "Thank you." She couldn't get over the amount of work John had put into preparing the farmhouse, especially the room Lily was supposed to use for her artwork.

Peace and quiet. Almost everything Lily could ever need, except for two things. A computer and her freedom.

* * * *

Michael pressed against the wall and listened carefully. The two speakers had moved through the house to a room close to the front and right-hand side. He frowned, able to make out a part of the conversation. Had John done something special for her? His jaw tightened at the thought. No doubt the asshole assumed anything he did was important to Lily. The damn man was in love with her, focused on her in a way that was both dangerous and sickening. What would John do when Lily refused to love him?

No, with Mags's help, Michael was going to get Lily out of there before it was too late.

Mags gestured to the window behind her. It was a large one that would let plenty of natural light into the room. She then pointed to the door and held up two fingers. Both Lily and John were in the room.

Michael reached for the door handle and tested it.

Not locked.

Mags edged closer to the window and looked inside, her movements quick and professional as she checked the room. Silently she turned and stepped toward the door, and in rapid signals, she indicated there were two people there, one door that led into the main body of the house and one other window at the side of the room.

Michael nodded and pointed to the door before he began the countdown. Even if they weren't charging in, Michael knew it was best if they entered together. He opened the door on the final count and tensed. If the hinges squeaked, it was over; John would be alerted to them entering, and Lily would be in immediate danger.

Nothing happened.

Thank God.

Michael's heart raced, but he kept himself calm and focused. Lily was there. If he let his emotions get the better of him, she would be hurt, perhaps killed. He couldn't risk it.

They slipped inside, cat-footed as they kept to the walls. Michael didn't need to check on Mags to know what she was doing. The woman was as skilled as he was, if not more so. The voices were clearer now, the words easier to make out.

"Lily, did I miss anything?" John's voice, eager and filled with hope.

"Not that I can think of, except a computer and scanner, but I understand why you don't want me to have either right now." Lily's voice was oddly calm.

What the hell is going on?

"Good, good. Remember you won't be working on commissions. All you have to do is create art for yourself. No pressure, no deadlines, only your art. The way it should always have been." John's voice moved closer to the door.

Michael looked at Mags and gestured to the opening, making it clear he was going to go to the other side. Mags shook her head, refusing to allow Michael to dart to the side. He scowled, but she was right. At this point, it was too risky. If John saw him, it would put Lily in danger.

Mags indicated the wall.

John was moving, at least according to his voice.

"I want you to be happy here, Lily. I know you can be. It's going to be wonderful once you've shaken off the taint Michael has left you with."

Mags inclined her head, the go-ahead given for Michael to move. He waited for a second, double-checking he had time before he made it to the other side of the door and Mags settled into the remaining side.

Where's Lily within the room? Still close to John?

"I'm impressed by everything you've put together, but I'm going to need time. Remember, I told you that. I'm still a bit shaken. You shot Daniel, and you still have a gun in your hand. It's scaring me, John. I don't like being scared."

Had she heard them, or was it pure dumb luck she'd let them know about the gun?

Mags gestured to the door. Michael nodded and readied himself. As one they burst into the room, Glocks at the ready.

"No!" John cried out and moved. The small gap between himself and Lily closed before Michael could react.

Lily was in the line of fire.

"You're not taking her from me. I won't let it happen."

Lily gasped as she was yanked back against John, the gun pointed at Michael and Mags. Even as Michael watched Lily, he could see the fear flickering across her eyes, and she tensed but didn't fight the hold.

"Put the gun down, John. We don't want anyone to get hurt here," Michael instructed.

"Only one who's going to get hurt is you," John warned, his teeth bared. "She's mine; she's always been mine. I've seen what you do to her, and I know she doesn't like it. She was meant to be here with me, but you walked in and forced her." He waved the gun at Michael and Mags, but the focus of his attention was Michael. "I bet you fucked this one as well, turned her into your willing little sex slave, and you tried to do the same thing with my Lily. My

Shadows of the Past

sweet, innocent Lily."

Sex slave? Shit. Had Lily told him something? Let it slip somehow?

"I don't know what you mean, John." Michael forced his voice to remain calm.

"I've never slept with Michael. I work with him, nothing more," Mags added, her gun trained on John. "Why don't you let Lily go, and we can all talk about this."

"She's mine. She wants to stay with me." John tugged Lily closer, the gun now focused on Mags.

Michael edged forward a step.

"Don't move. I mean it. Don't you fucking move." John swung the gun back to Michael. His finger tightened on the trigger even as Lily moved. She slammed her heel back into John's shin and slammed her bound hands up into John's arm.

The gun, still held in John's hands, jerked upward even as the shot rang out. Michael felt something smack into his shoulder, but he reacted, gun trained on John. A single shot from his Glock before he stumbled back, aware of the blow that had struck his body and the burning pain that followed.

"Michael!" Lily's voice broke through the pain as he forced himself to stand up.

Was she hurt? He had to get to her.

Mags had moved. She no longer stood near him but had John on the floor, his arms yanked behind his back.

Shit, Michael cursed under his breath as pain burned through his shoulder. He sat down, hard. His legs splayed out as he tried to force his mind to work. This didn't make sense. It wasn't a severe wound. He'd been clipped, right? Like any good hero, a flesh wound he could shake off?

Right, and this is the point where I sweep Lily into my arms and claim her with a passionate kiss.

"Oh God, you're bleeding." Delicate hands pressed against his shoulder. "It's bad. We need to get you to a doctor."

Well, didn't that just suck?

Shadows of the Past

Chapter Fifteen

Lily paced across the waiting room, her gaze flicking back and forth between the clock and the door. The door she hoped the doctor would walk in through. It had all happened too fast. The two of them appearing in the room, the shots. Mags and Michael. Michael stumbling back, blood everywhere as Mags subdued John, but all Lily could think about at that moment was Michael.

She glanced down at the scrubs she'd been given. All of her clothing had been taken for processing, evidence for when the case came to court. If it went that far. Maybe, if she were lucky, John would confess, and it would all be finished with.

"Ms. Elliot, we need to sit down. There's a lot we need to go over."

Lily tensed at the voice and turned. Detective Richmond stood in the middle of the doorway and smiled as he gestured to the chairs. Without a word, she turned and walked back to a seat she had semi-claimed as her own. How long had she been waiting now? Two hours? More?

"The doctors have given you a clean bill of health." Keith Richmond settled into a chair opposite Lily. "But I guess you feel as far from normal as possible right now, after the events of the day."

Lily ducked her head and wrapped her arms around her body. She didn't want to be here. She needed to be with Michael, but they hadn't brought him back from surgery yet. She could barely recall what had been said, something about an artery being nicked, but had that been all? There had to be more going on given the length of time they'd been working on him. She shivered and hugged herself a little more. "I'm cold."

"Shock or adrenaline drop. It's normal, but you need to stay warm. I don't want you ending up in a room here." Richmond rose and moved to the doorway. A moment later he flagged down a nurse. It didn't take long before there was a blanket wrapped around Lily and a hot drink pressed into her hands.

Lily sat there, her gaze now fixed on the steam as it rose from the cup. "Sorry, I don't know what happened there. It's all so weird."

"I understand, but I need you to go over what you remember. Take it slow. I'm right here, and I already have the statement from the other witness. Margaret Armati. I believe she works with Mr. Parker?"

Lily nodded. She didn't know anything about the other woman, not really. "Mags. Michael called her Mags."

"Yes, she mentioned that." Richmond looked over his notes. "We'll do this one step at a time, and we'll take as many breaks as you think you need. I'm in no hurry."

The idea of going over everything made Lily's stomach roll, but it had to be done. John had been arrested, and statements would be needed. Court cases, lawyers, statements, questions, it would never end. Lily took a deep breath, and she did her best to recall the details of what had happened with careful nudging from Richmond. By the time she was done, Lily was trembling as she tried to keep herself calm, but it was over, and she met Richmond's gaze. "Thank you for being patient with me."

Richmond patted her hand and smiled. "I'm only sorry we couldn't stop him before it reached this point. I wanted to be able to do more."

"But it wasn't your call. I understand resources and the fact the request had to go up the chain. With no idea of who was behind the stalking, getting a temporary restraining order wasn't on the cards." It sat ill with Lily, but there was nothing she could or wanted to do about it right now. Not when all she wanted was to find out how Michael was doing and when she would be allowed to see him again.

"He's going to remain in custody for some time. The odds are he'll have to go through a psych evaluation, but you'll be safe now."

Lily wanted to believe the man, as it was the only way she was holding onto her sanity.

Shadows of the Past

"Do you need a ride home?"

"No, I'm staying right here."

A figure stepped into the doorway, and for a moment Lily hoped it was the doctor, but a tall dark-haired woman with olive skin stood there.

"Mags?"

The woman smiled. "Yes, we haven't met officially yet, but I figured now the cops were done with me, I could come and sit with you. If that's all right?" Mags turned her brown eyes on the detective and smiled.

"I'm on my way out. We're all done here." Richmond rose from his seat and pressed one hand on Lily's for a moment. "Call me if you need me or remember something else."

"I will." Not that she thought anything else could be added to the statement, but stranger things had happened.

Mags settled into the seat next to Lily. "He's going to pull through. Michael's a tough one. He's not going to give up, not when he has you to look forward to."

Lily snorted. "Like that's enough to help him. There's no need to patronize me."

Mags turned in her chair and caught Lily by the chin, her voice hard, eyes narrowed. "The last thing I'd do is patronize you or any other woman, Lily. I want you to listen to me."

Lily winced but didn't pull away. "Okay."

"Michael loves you, and love is damned powerful. It gives you a reason to hold on, and that's what Michael will do." Mags let go of Lily's jaw. "You're going to be together again, and what you do from there is up to you."

What they did? Lily closed her eyes and let the tension ease from her shoulders. He had to pull through. There was no other choice. She didn't want to think about life without him. No, the very idea of losing Michael left Lily cold to the core. "I need him."

"I know."

A noise in the corridor silenced the conversation as Lily lifted her gaze, searching the doorway for any sign of a doctor. This time one appeared, still in his surgical scrubs, mask hanging down around his throat, the cap in place. "Ms. Elliot?"

"Yes." She rose, her heart pounding in her chest.

"Mr. Parker pulled through, Ms. Elliot. He's a fighter."

"What happened?" Mags was at Lily's side, one arm wrapped around Lily's shoulders.

"Artery was nicked by the bullet, which is why he was losing so much blood, and in the process, a previous injury was aggravated. It could have been a lot worse, but fortunately, the paramedics were able to get the bleeding under control. Because of that, he was stable when we got him into surgery."

It had been a rush, Lily recalled. Pure chaos after the shooting, with the police and paramedics arriving on the scene minutes after Michael had been hit. If that hadn't been the case, she now understood Michael might not have made it. She swallowed down her fear. "Will I be able to see him?"

"Yes, soon enough. Mr. Parker's in recovery now and will be moved to a room shortly. We'll let you know which room as soon as he's settled."

* * * *

Michael didn't move—he couldn't, not at first—as he stared up at the tiled ceiling. He'd come to earlier, several times on and off when he'd been in the recovery room, and vaguely remembered being moved to a private room, but he must have passed out again not long after being settled in. Now, as he stared at the off-white tiles, he tried to move again and winced as his body told him it hadn't been the wisest choice.

Surgery. Yes, he'd been under the knife. Fine, he'd half expected it after being shot. A doctor or nurse, he couldn't remember which, had told him what had happened, but all he could think about when the pain meds didn't fog his mind beyond reason was Lily.

She hadn't been hurt, had she? He frowned and tried to sort through his memories about the events that had led up to and im-

Shadows of the Past

mediately followed the shooting. No, he couldn't remember anything to indicate she'd been hurt. Bound and terrified, yes, but not injured.

"Michael?" Lily's voice drew his attention to the doorway.

His Lily stood there in clean scrubs. Had they taken her clothing for processing? Now she wore a set of scrubs that made his fingers itch with the need to push them up out of the way.

"Oh, God, Lily." His throat thickened and he shook his head. "I'm sorry. I should never have let you go into the office on your own."

Lily darted across to the side of the bed and paused before she carefully wrapped one arm around him. Only then did he realize his injured shoulder still hurt despite the pain meds, and his arm had been placed in a sling, no doubt to reduce pulling on his injury. "It wasn't your fault. I told you that you couldn't go in with me. It was my decision."

"Yes, I know, but I'm your damned security. I should have overridden you and gone in anyway. At least you wouldn't have been snatched by John." He inhaled the scent of her hair and smiled, his uninjured arm wrapped around her shoulder. She was here, alive and in his arms.

"He'd have found a way to snatch me later on, maybe when you returned home or at an event. It was going to happen sooner or later. Better it happened when you were around. Don't you think?" She turned enough in his arms to press a tender kiss against his chin before she pulled back and sat on the edge of the bed. "You scared me."

"You kinda did the same thing to me." Fear, yeah. He could admit to being afraid when he'd known she'd been taken. Shit, terrified was closer to the mark. "Let's not go there again. No more being kidnapped, got it?"

"Not on my to-do list." Lily smiled and reached for his good hand, tangling her fingers with his. "But your work..." She faltered.

"Yes, it means I might run into something like this again," he admitted and tightened his hold on Lily's hand. "I wish I could say I'll never be hurt again, but I can't promise that." This wasn't the first time he'd been hurt because of work, and he doubted it would be the last, but what if this was too much for Lily? Doubt settled into place, a heavy weight that pressed against his heart. He had to say it, had to give her the choice to walk away, even if it killed him. "If this life, the one I live, is too much for you, I'll understand. God, I don't want to lose you, but I won't force you to stay."

Lily tensed, wet her bottom lip, and turned away, her eyes half closed.

This was it. She was going to leave. Michael couldn't blame her. Very few people could live with the fact their spouse or lover could be shot or killed in the line of duty. How many divorces had taken place in law enforcement families or the military because of the strain? Hell if he knew. He wouldn't stop her if she needed to leave, needed to walk away instead of dealing with the potential for pain that came with his life.

Shouldn't have given her my heart; shouldn't have let myself love or care for her. I've done this to myself.

Did he even deserve happiness or a woman like Lily after what had happened with Ophelia?

With a sigh, Lily turned to look at him before she pressed her free hand against his cheek, her touch soft and warm. "I wouldn't ask you to give up your career, no more than you've asked me to give up mine, and if it means there are times when I end up sitting at your side as you heal, or waiting for you to come home, then so be it. I'm not saying I'm going to handle it well, or there won't be nights that I cry and shake, but I'm not going to turn away from you because of your work." She leaned in and pressed her lips against his, the kiss gentle but filled with a passion neither his mind nor his body could deny.

His cock thickened despite the pain and drugs in his system as he groaned against her lips. "I need you."

"Not here, love, and not now." She pulled back, her hand still against his cheek. "But soon, I promise you as soon as you're out

Shadows of the Past

of here and the doctor has given you medical clearance, then I'm yours. In any way you want me, I'm yours."

"Do you still want to move to be closer to me?" He had to know, had to understand what they agreed to.

"Yes, always. And when we're ready, we move in together," Lily agreed, her eyes dancing with joy. "It's what we both need, what we want. I'm not about to run from you, Michael. You're stuck with me now."

Stuck with her. Yeah, he could live with that. "Even though I'm going to walk you into the darkness with me, introduce you to all the kinky things I enjoy?" He had to know, had to put all the pieces together and make sure there wasn't a sliver of doubt for either of them.

"Yes, even then I'll walk willingly with you into the darkness."

Michael's heart sang as he pulled Lily down into a full kiss, his lips claiming hers as the remaining doubts and the last shadow of Ophelia faded into the background. He was, at that moment, despite being in a hospital bed, finally home.